秘 WARNED

# Other Mei-hua Adventures

*Hidden*
*A Mei-hua Adventure*

*Lotus Shoes*
*A Short Story from Ancient China*

## Coming Soon

*Trapped*
*A Mei-hua Adventure*

To discover more stories
about ancient China visit
**padevoe.com.**

A Mei-hua Adventure

# P.A. De Voe

Drum
Tower
Press
St. Louis, Missouri

First Edition. First Printing, 2015

Printed in the United States of America

Publisher's Note
This is a work of fiction. Names, characters, places, and incidents either are the product of the author's imagination or are used fictitiously.

Cover design by Kelly Cochran

Library of Congress Control Number: 2015913883
Published by
Drum Tower Press, LLC
165 Bon Chateau Drive
Saint Louis, Missouri 63141-6081
http://padevoe.com/?page_id=177

ISBN-10: 1942667035
ISBN-13: 978-1-942667-03-2

# DEDICATION

To my patient and supportive family.

Thank you.

# ACKNOWLEDGEMENTS

I want to give a big thank you to those who read through the early versions of the manuscript and made helpful suggestions and comments: my fellow Sisters in Crime Guppy member, Andrew MacRae, who was my manuscript critique partner; my husband Ron, who gamely read through several versions; and, of course, my indomitable editor Renée DeVoe Mertz.

As always, any errors in this novel are mine alone.

## Primary Characters

This second story in the Mei-hua trilogy is set in 1380 China, the beginning of the Ming Dynasty.

| | |
|---|---|
| Da-shan | Former ruffian, now a Buddhist monk |
| Doctor Lum | An Imperially trained doctor |
| Hsu Ping-an | Mei-hua's friend; Mei-hua lives with her and her family |
| Hsu Guei-lung | Ping-an's brother |
| Madam Wu | Ping-an and Guei-lung's mother; married to Master Hsu |
| Master Hsu | Mei-hua's father's friend; married to Madam Wu; Ping-an and Guei-lung's father |
| Mr. Mien | Noodle vendor |
| Mr. Mu | Carpenter |
| Mrs. Mu | Carpenter's wife |
| Soldier Guo | Mei-hua's guard |
| Zhang Mei-hua | Our heroine; temporary ward of Master Hsu and Madam Wu |

# CHAPTER 1

MEI-HUA, COMFORTABLE and slightly bored, munched on dried plums and drank tea with Ping-an. The two girls enjoyed a mid-morning snack as they sat on the large, raised kang, quietly talking and laughing. A maid had placed their wooden tea tray with its four stumpy legs on the edge of the kang, giving the girls plenty of room to lounge against a pile of pillows.

Another maid slipped into the room and announced that Mrs. Mu, the carpenter's wife, had arrived and would like to see Mei-hua. Mei-hua flashed a delighted smile at Ping-an, who grinned back. Mrs. Mu was a special friend to Mei-hua and always welcome by all within the household.

"Bring her in," Mei-hua said.

The maid instantly left and returned shortly, leading the elderly woman. At the sight of her friend, Mei-hua covered her mouth in dismay, shocked at how much she'd aged in the one short week since she'd seen her last. The newcomer's face resembled a worn and distressed piece of crinkled cloth. She moved forward as if trudging through ankle-deep mud.

As soon as the desolate woman raised her eyes and recognized Mei-hua sitting next to Ping-an, she ran up to the kang and fell on her knees, crying. Loose strands of grey hair clung to her wet cheeks.

"Mei-hua! You must help us. Mr. Mu is dying!"

Mei-hua and Ping-an sprang from the kang and wrapped their arms around the sorrowful figure folded on the floor in front of them.

"How awful! What happened?" Ping-an exclaimed as she released the sobbing woman and leaned back to examine her more fully."Please don't cry, Mrs. Mu!" Mei-hua said. "How can Mr. Mu be dying? Just last week he was laughing and teasing me." The words spilled out as she loosened her grip on Mrs. Mu's shoulders and grasped her hands together in her own.

"Yes, as you say, he was fine, even happy," Mrs. Mu began, her voice quivering. "I don't know why he got sick. Perhaps he works too hard." She stopped for a moment, nodding to herself, thinking of the long hours he spent in his carpenter's shop. Even though he employed several laborers as assistants, he always started before daybreak and worked long after dark.

Continuing her story as the girls drew her up onto the kang to sit near them, she said, "Shortly after your last visit ... you know he always so looks forward to your visits. They are among the few times he will stop working and relax." Moving a wrinkled, weathered hand across her eyes, she pushed away tears threatening to slide down her cheeks. Mei-hua murmured encouragement for her to go on.

Starting again, Mrs. Mu said, "Well, he began to complain about his chest hurting and sometimes his arms and hands tingled, making it too difficult for him to hold a chisel or a hammer. Work became impossible."

"Has he seen a doctor yet?" Mei-hua asked. Even

though he had many customers, the couple had little money. They were unlikely to waste it on the expense of a doctor and medicine if they could avoid it.

"Yes, yes. Mr. Mien, the noodle stall owner—you remember him, he has his cart right outside our door— recommended a local doctor. The doctor came right away. The first thing he did was to tell my husband to stop working, to rest, and then he gave him some very expensive medicine." She quickly added, "I don't begrudge the expense. No, no. His health is all that matters.

"We've done everything the doctor told us. Plus, he comes every day, personally bringing Mr. Mu his daily dose of medicine. But nothing good has come of it, even though it costs a lot of money. Just the opposite. Each day, my husband gets worse. He has difficultly holding up his head and seems to be in a lot of pain.

"You know, Mei-hua," Mrs. Mu dropped her voice and looked directly into her young friend's eyes. "I don't trust that doctor any more. What good has he done? All these days, all his treatments, at such an expense, and Mr. Mu keeps getting worse." She paused. Tears again welled in her eyes.

The two girls bent over the despairing woman, murmuring in sympathy.

"When my mother-in-law died she was under the care of a local doctor," Mrs. Mu noted with a trace of bitterness. "They're not well trained. Many are not honest, taking advantage of the poor and dying. Her doctor never went to the national medical school, never took the imperial medical examinations. He apprenticed under a street doctor for a few years, that's all." She sighed. "Just like this man treating my Mr. Mu. He may be good, or not. I don't know. My mother-in-law was a wonderful woman who was good to me. We paid a lot of money for her care, but she died anyway. Now, I'm afraid my husband will die too." Her voice rose to a wail.

Mei-hua and Ping-an again closed around Mrs. Mu, comforting her as she continued to pour out her misery.

The noise brought in Ping-an's mother's servant, Lotus Blossom. Recognizing Mrs. Mu, she insisted the girls explain the problem. Her job was to report back to Ping-an's mother on everything that happened in the house.

In retelling the story, Mei-hua added how important it was for Mr. Mu to be seen by an imperial doctor because Mrs. Mu wasn't sure his present doctor was competent enough. No sooner had she finished, then Lotus Blossom rushed out to inform Madam Wu.

Mei-hua had little faith in the local doctors. These specialists were called bell-doctors because they walked through the streets clanging a bell to let people know they were coming. She recognized the need for their work when dealing with everyday, common illnesses. Their education came from working as an apprentice for years under another bell-doctor. As a result, their medical knowledge and training could be excellent, good, or not so good. Without the rigors of formal schooling and being certified, bell-doctors were only as knowledgeable and competent as their often haphazard training and scruples led them to be.

Mr. and Mrs. Mu had done a lot for her. Truly, she owed her present security to them. They had saved her from a life of hiding as an unknown, orphaned street person. And, ultimately, they gave her the courage to return to Magistrate Hsu and Madam Wu's household, where she now lived with Ping-an and her family.

She had to help the Mus in every way possible. And, in this case, she believed only an imperially trained and licensed doctor should treat Mr. Mu. Such physicians, however, were extraordinarily expensive and the average person would have a difficult time paying such fees. Another problem was that they usually only treated clients recommended to them by other patrons. She had made a point to stress the importance of getting an imperial doctor to Lotus Blossom, for she had no doubt Madam Wu, as the wife of a magistrate, would be able to hire the best doctor to send over to the Mus' modest home.

After Lotus Blossom left the room, Mei-hua turned to Mrs. Mu again, "Please, don't worry, we'll get the best treatment for Mr. Mu. And don't worry about the cost." She promised this last without the authority to do so, although she was confident Ping-an's kindly parents would help this couple to whom she herself owed so much. "I am sure he'll soon be well again."

"Thank you, Mei-hua. Thank you both," Mrs. Mu said softly. Grasping Mei-hua's hand, she continued, "You are such a help to us. If you were our own daughter, you couldn't do more." Before she could continue with a flood of gratitude, Mei-hua gently released the woman's grip and, picking up a cup of tea, she pressed it into the older woman's hands.

"Please stay and drink a little tea with Ping-an, you'll feel better soon." Mei-hua said rising from the kang.

Realizing Mei-hua intended to leave, Mrs. Mu stared at her young friend. "Where ...?"

"I'll be right back. I'm going to change into street clothing so I can go back to your house with you. It won't take long."

Although Mrs. Mu protested, saying Mei-hua didn't need to come to the shop, Mei-hua insisted. Then, leaving her in Ping-an's hands, she went into her own room to change out of her silk yellow-on-sky-blue jacket and flowing blue pants. Her maid helped her slip into a pair of plain yellow trousers and an unassuming, long, cotton jacket with a dark blue-on-blue geometric pattern. By the time she returned, she found that Madam Wu, Ping-an's mother, and Guei-lung, Ping-an's brother, had joined them. Guei-lung wore the long grey robe he usually put on when he went out of the house.

"Mei-hua," Madam Wu began as soon as she'd entered the room, "Ping-an tells me you intend to go back with Mrs. Mu. Good. It's right that you should help them.

"Your father and my husband are like brothers and, therefore, when your father found himself in trouble and needed to send you away for protection, we were a natural choice. Here, pretending to be our own niece, you are able to remain safely hidden within our family." Madam Wu spread her hands out and around as if taking in the entire house and those in it.

Mei-hua stood near the kang, not daring to sit or to look at Madam Wu, afraid that Ping-an's mother was preparing to say she couldn't leave. If Madam Wu did demand that she remain, how could Mei-hua help the

Mus from the women's quarters in the Hsu household?

Ping-an's mother continued as if not noticing Mei-hua's unease. "Fate used Mr. and Mrs. Mu to bring you to us. You—and we—owe them much."

Mei-hua glanced up at the elegant woman, a note of hope danced in her heart.

Madam Wu shook her head. "However, don't think you can sweep out of the house, go traipsing through the public streets, and all will be well. That's impossible."

Mei-hua couldn't hold back the disappointment. This time Madam Wu noticed her reaction. She pursed her lips, then said, "No," as if answering an unspoken question from her young charge. "You may go, but not alone."

Mei-hua's heart fluttered and she shot a look at Mrs. Mu who remained a stone figure on the kang, listening to every word.

"Master Hsu assigned a soldier to accompany you as a guard. From now on, he'll remain with you whenever you go outside our compound. His duty is to protect you," Madam Wu finished.

"Is it Li Chi?" Guei-Lung asked, referring to the Captain of the Guards.

"Li Chi is on another mission for your father. The soldier assigned to this duty has recently joined Master Hsu and the court." After a pause and as if apologizing for not having a more seasoned soldier, she added, "He has been highly recommended for this position."

Turning back to Mei-hua, she continued, "Strictly speaking, he is not your personal servant. Still, if you need anything, you can depend on him.

"I also want Guei-lung to go along with you. Since your father and Master Hsu are as close as brothers, you are a member of our family and our responsibility. It is not proper for a young woman to be traveling through the public streets without an escort. Therefore, Guei-lung will also accompany you whenever you are outside the protection of our home. And, of course, he will remain at Mr. and Mrs. Mu's home for as long as you do.

"Don't worry," she raised her hand to silence Mei-hua's protests even before she made them. "He can stay as long as is necessary. Clearly this is a serious affair and requires our full support. With so many strangers coming into and going out of the Mu house, you must have someone with you. As a matter of fact, when I was trying to think of whom to send, Guei-lung volunteered."

Guei-lung smiled and bowed to Mei-hua at these last words.

Pleased, but without smiling back, Mei-hua nodded her head to acknowledge the bow. It would be unseemly to appear too enthusiastic at the prospect of his going with her. For, although the Hsu family considered Guei-lung to be her paternal cousin, and, therefore, like a brother, they were not really blood relatives. A fact Mei-hua was all too aware of whenever they were together.

And, while Mei-hua didn't think it was necessary to have so many extra people accompany her, she appreciated his mother's concern, especially since it meant Guei-lung would travel with her. They hadn't had a chance talk in quite a while. They lived in the same household, yet days could pass without their seeing each other. His studies kept him busy in his rooms, and Mei-hua was largely confined to the women's quarters.

Madam Wu nodded toward the door. "I've sent a servant to Doctor Lum's home telling him of the urgency of this case. He should be at the house shortly. "

Madam Wu scanned Mei-hua's clothing. "I see you're dressed. Take Mrs. Mu home, stay with her, and send word back after Doctor Lum has had a chance to examine Mr. Mu."

She turned to Mrs. Mu, who was trying to thank her, and gently said, "You and your husband have done so much for our Mei-hua and her family. We all owe you an immense debt. Please, allow us to send Doctor Lum over to care for Mr. Mu as a small token of our appreciation."

Perhaps, in other times, Mrs. Mu's pride would have made her fight such generosity. But with her husband dying before her very eyes, all she could do was thank Madam Wu over and over again. The elderly carpenter's wife was well aware there was no way an imperial doctor would come to their humble home without the sponsorship of a family such as the Hsu's. This was no time for false pride.

In spite of the closeness of the carpenter's house to the Hsu compound, etiquette demanded Mei-hua, as a member of a magistrate's family, travel in a palanquin. Guei-lung insisted on walking and joined a young soldier standing in front of the palanquin ready to lead the small group to the Mus' home.

Pausing at the carrier's side as the servants

helped Mrs. Mu enter first, Mei-hua eagerly took in the street scene. The air was saturated with the scent of salty and sweet foods. A cacophony of sound permeated the area as the peddlers cried out to passers-by. Laborers sloped down the wide street. Their feet skimmed over the top of the road and their muscled, sinewy arms balanced heavy loads swinging from poles pressing into their shoulders. A group of street urchins dashed around a corner and disappeared, their high-pitched voices lingering behind. Several beggars threaded slowly through the crowds, looking for alms.

Turning back to her little entourage, Mei-hua scrutinized the soldier next to Guei-lung. Her first impression was how, with his slender build, he appeared much younger than the other soldiers stationed at the magistrate's office.

The youthful soldier stood listening to Guei-lung, responding with short, quick nods of his head, his oval face defined by a well shaped jaw line. An inexplicable half dimple on his left cheek caught Mei-hua's eye. She studied his face a few more seconds, reflecting on how his strong black eyebrows appeared to have been drawn with an ink brush. Suddenly he looked up and stared back at her. Startled, since soldiers and other servants never looked directly into the eyes of their masters and mistresses, she quickly glanced away and then back, just in time to catch a twinkle in his dark brown eyes and a small grin tugging at his mouth.

*How odd*, she thought, dropping her gaze once more. *Why does he seem so brazen?* She shook her head as she entered the enclosed carrier, thinking again of how the young soldier appeared to skirt the edges of impertinence. Once seated, Mei-hua pushed the curtain next to her aside and continued to observe her surroundings as they left the Hsu's front gate. The palanquin stopped again almost immediately. A ragged beggar with a scraggly beard appeared in the middle of the street. He leaned heavily on an iron crutch and appeared to be unaware of Mei-hua's caravan, making it impossible for them to move forward.

Guei-lung strode toward the cripple and, glowering at him, demanded he move aside and let the palanquin pass. The beggar, though stooped over, nevertheless looked straight at Guei-lung without replying or moving.

"What the ...?" Guei-lung sputtered. "What are you doing? Get out of the way! Don't you see we are trying to get through?" Nothing Guei-lung said had any affect.

Listening to Guei-lung order the beggar aside, she finally pushed the curtain back even further and stuck her head out of the small window. Peering at the bent, crippled man who halted their small party, she noticed he carried a bottle gourd in his free hand. He seemed insignificant standing there in front of Guei-lung, yet, for all the young man's ordering and demanding, the cripple remained unmoved.

No sooner had she stuck her head out the window when the beggar faced her directly and said, "What is true may seem false and what is false may seem true. Look into your heart to find the truth. However," here he paused to point straight at Mei-hua, "if you don't recognize the truth, death will result."

# CHAPTER 2

AS HE FINISHED SPEAKING, the beggar turned and started to limp away, leaving Mei-hua staring and Guei-lung sputtering after him. With a momentary look at Mei-hua, Guei-lung scowled in exasperation before turning back a second later to again berate the beggar. But the cripple was gone; he'd disappeared, almost as if he'd never been there.

"What do you make of that?" Mei-hua asked.

"Just a crazy, drunk vagrant," Guei-lung answered. "That gourd he carried probably had wine in it. Even though we're in a new, enlightened Dynasty, there are still too many of these people around. That's why I'm here: to protect you from that type." He drew himself up to his full height, glancing to the left and right as if to chase away any other potential vagabonds.

"Guard," he ordered, "keep the road clear for Mistress Zhang's palanquin!"

The young soldier—who had been standing by and casually watching with that suspicious twinkle in his eyes—snapped to attention, holding his spear at a 45 degree angle in front of him.

Mei-hua hid a smile. Clearly, Guei-lung had not prevented the beggar from doing what he wanted. He stood in the street, stopped her palanquin, calmly called out his strange message, and left on his own terms. She was glad to have Guei-lung's company on this trip, but she felt perfectly capable of "protecting" herself. Then, glancing at the soldier standing at attention, she thought he looked more amused than formidable. Mei-hua felt he would not offer much protection either.

"Did you hear what he said?" Mei-hua asked Guei-lung.

"Something about truth and dying. Just the kind of mumble-jumble you'd expect."

"Really?" Mei-hua responded absently. She tried to remember the vagrant's words: "What is true may seem false and what is false may seem true. Look into your heart to find the truth, for if you don't recognize the truth, death will result." It sounded like a warning. Most beggars ask for food or money, not talk about truth and dying and then disappear before getting any alms. This one was unusual. At the same time, he seemed familiar in an odd sort of way. Had she seen him before? Mei-hua shook her head. No. She would have remembered.

As Mei-hua ruminated over this street scene, Mrs. Mu broke into her reverie. "What's the matter? Why've we stopped in the middle of the street? We need to hurry back to the shop. I have to take care of Mr. Mu, to be sure he's all right."

Mei-hua nodded her head. Of course, Mrs. Mu was anxious to get back; they must not delay any longer.

"Guei-lung, can we pass now? Mrs. Mu needs to be with her husband and we should be at the house when the doctor arrives."

Guei-lung raised his hand in agreement, turned, and continued forward. Striding slightly behind the soldier, he led the palanquin through the crowded street to the carpenter's shop where Mr. Mu lay dying in the back room.

When the carriers stopped again, Mei-hua pushed the curtain open to discover that they'd reached their destination and had stopped in front of the shop. The servants helped Mrs. Mu out of the chair first, and Mei-hua followed. Stepping down onto the dusty street, she saw Mrs. Mu walk up to her front door where Guei-lung stood with a man in a dingy apron. Mei-hua recognized the fellow as Mr. Mien, the noodle stall owner. He appeared to be as greasy and as unsavory as his soup. But, Mei-hua cautioned herself, appearances could be deceiving. After all, he was the one who found a doctor for Mr. Mu, and Mrs. Mu seemed to rely on him. Even as Mei-hua's instincts rankled at the sight of the man, her mind told her to trust Mrs. Mu, who she believed to be a good judge of character. For the sake of her friend, then, Mei-hua would try to be nice and not judge Mr. Mien too harshly.

Catching up to Mrs. Mu and Guei-lung, Mei-hua heard the noodle vendor exclaim in his ingratiating voice, "Oh, how wonderful! You have been able to get an imperial doctor to come and treat Mr. Mu. Of course, the local doctor I recommended," he said, stressing the last two words before continuing, "could never ..."

Mrs. Mu hurriedly interrupted him, "Thank you, thank you, for all you have done. The bell-doctor's been wonderful, of course! Both Mr. Mu and I are truly grateful for everything you've done for us. But what could I do? The Hsu family insisted on this other doctor also examining him.

"It's only because Mr. Mu's health is deteriorating so rapidly that I even considered having someone new come in. Please don't be offended, Mr. Mien. We both are thankful for your help in our time of need."

Mei-hua listened to Mrs. Mu's formal exclamations of thanks—given, she knew, so Mr. Mien's feelings wouldn't be hurt. For the sake of her husband's well-being, no one must think unkind or bad thoughts about the sick person. Such thoughts were bad luck and could further damage the person's health, even hasten his death. Mrs. Mu's entire recital was an attempt to keep away the bad luck which might strike the carpenter if Mr. Mien thought the couple was ungrateful for his assistance. Bad luck was always waiting to destroy good fortune or make an already difficult situation worse.

The noodle vendor still stood like a guard in front of the entrance, alternately wiping his hands on his apron stiffened with grime and passing his right hand over his stringy hair. "Well, well, Mrs. Mu, I am sure you did not mean to doubt the local doctor's ability. Naturally, you must accept Magistrate Hsu's help. I am only too happy your good husband's getting the best care money can buy." Mr. Mien gave her a gloomy smile.

Stepping aside, he added, "If there is anything else I can do, I am always here." He waved his left hand toward his noodle stall. Then, as if just recognizing Mei-hua, he gushed with the same cheerless smile, "Zhang Mei-hua, how glad I am to see you here, to finally come and assist the people who have done so much for you."

Mei-hua didn't miss the implication she'd been delinquent in her duties toward Mr. and Mrs. Mu, but she resolved to ignore the comments of this irritating little insect of a man. Mrs. Mu's strong conviction about the power of harsh words or negative thoughts to damage Mr. Mu's critical condition even further constrained Mei-hua. So, she merely smiled and bowed toward Mr. Mien. Being much younger than the noodle vendor, as well as being a girl, required nothing beyond this polite show of respect.

She straightened up and caught the mirthful eye of the young soldier as he quietly came up to stand near her. Was he protecting her? From what? She looked away, but not before taking him in again with another quick glance. He did not look like most soldiers she'd seen and certainly not like any soldier of rank. He was too young, too slender, slightly bow-legged, and had an air of irreverence. And what about the perpetual smile which constantly tugged at the corner of his mouth? Before Mei-hua had a chance to consider this strange new guard, Mrs. Mu took her arm and began walking toward the door.

Passing the obsequious vendor, they entered the dim, sweet smelling carpenter's shop. Mrs. Mu stopped near piles of camphor, sandalwood, and planks of fir. She pulled Mei-hua even closer and whispered in her ear, "Sometimes we don't really understand the inner nature of people. Especially those who are very different from ourselves."

Mei-hua felt her face get hot. Mrs. Mu could tell she didn't like the noodle vendor and was attempting to correct her attitude.

"Mr. Mien is rough and often difficult, but his life has not been easy. Less than two years ago his small restaurant burned down. He not only lost his business, but both his wife and ten year old son died in the fire. He had no choice but to start over again. Today all he has is a simple noodle stand."

"I'm sorry, Mrs. Mu ...," Mei-hua began.

The elderly woman patted her arm. "I know. I know. You have a good heart and want to do what is right by my husband and me. All I'm saying is that Mr. Mien understands suffering and loss. He wants to help us. Maybe it is his way of building good karma, I don't know." She lifted her tired eyes and looked around at the piles of wood and unfinished projects scattered throughout the room. "You've never liked him, even when you lived with us. But, for Mr. Mu's sake, show him respect."

Mei-hua's heart sank. This was the most serious rebuke from Mrs. Mu she had ever had. Could her instincts be so wrong? Still, she had to do as her friend said. She ducked her head and nodded a silent agreement.

Mrs. Mu resumed walking and Mei-hua followed, comforted by the sweet, familiar scents of the various woods lining the shop's walls. The window in the back room, which was both the kitchen and sleeping area, had been shuttered, darkening the space against the light of day. In the shadows, Mei-hua could make out Mr. Mu's figure as he lay in a quiet, deep sleep. Except for his motionless body, no one was about.

At the bell-doctor's recommendation, Mrs. Mu had sent the workers away in order to maintain a tranquil silence. Mei-hua understood what this silence cost the hard-working couple. Although she knew Mrs. Mu would do whatever the doctor said, she was also keenly aware that without workers filling the orders for caskets and furniture the couple had no income. Certainly, their bills must be growing, even as their savings kept dwindling. Mei-hua wondered how much longer it would be before the Mus would be in serious financial difficulties.

The older woman took a stool close to her husband and sat, shoulders slumped, waiting for him to wake. An unfinished bowl of noodle soup remained abandoned on the floor next to the bed. The local doctor had ordered only broth and noodles for his patient, saying the soup would make him stronger and enable him to overcome his sickness. Rice would not do; he must have noodles for a long life. Much to Mrs. Mu's relief, as soon as Mr. Mien learned what the local doctor prescribed, he volunteered to bring in a bowl each day. Even Mei-hua had to admit this was a great kindness on his part. Being a Southerner, Mrs. Mu had never made noodles and had little money right now to buy any. Mr. Mien's unexpected charity had averted a crisis for her.

Watching the bed-ridden carpenter and his wife, Mei-hua thought how old and vulnerable they appeared. Not at all like the picture of the strong, determined couple she carried in her heart.

Unable to suppress the melancholy which was slowly taking over her thoughts, Mei-hua walked out of the room and into the shop. The young guard followed her, keeping a slight distance between them. He was close enough to be a presence, but not intrude upon her space. Mei-hua stood near the half-opened front door, gazing at people walking past the shop or going into the temple across the street. Each person had his or her own private life and private worries. None were aware of the tragedy happening right here in this little corner of the great Hangzhou City.

Remaining in the comforting shade, Mei-hua leaned against the inside door jamb, observing the street scene. Mr. Mien served customers at his noodle stall. When a young boy of about ten cut across the street, the noodle vendor watched him. Mei-hua wondered if he was remembering his son. But then Mr. Mien turned sharply away and back toward his customers. He laughed and talked to a couple of tough-looking men lounging on his stools. One of the men pointed to a covered kettle of soup. Mr. Mien opened the lid and ladled out two bowls for them. She grimaced as he wiped his hands up and down the sides of his greasy apron before ladling out their meal.

Occasionally, he glanced in Mei-hua's direction, although apparently he did not notice her standing in the doorway's thick shadow. After handing over the two bowls to the strangers, Mr. Mien brought around another stool to join them. The men sat facing the temple, their backs to Mei-hua.

Watching this scene, Mei-hua thought about how many times she had stood just like this when she worked as an apprentice for Mr. Mu. She inhaled deeply, drawing in the sweet mix of the surrounding woods. How often she had swept piles of sawdust as the carpenter and his workers produced exquisite pieces of furniture and coffins for customers.

She smiled at the memory. It was only a few weeks ago, but it seemed like a lifetime.

Mei-hua took in the street scene again. She had often watched people buy a bowl of noodle soup and eat it while standing either singly or in groups near the stall. She always wondered how people managed to stomach his soup with the grease swimming thickly on the top of the broth. Mr. Mien sold the unappetizing mess as a pork and noodle soup. She shook her head. Implying there was any pork in the dish was more imagination than reality.

As the men put the bowls to their mouths and drank the soup, a nagging sensation caused Mei-hua to stare harder at the innocent scene. What bothered her? True, those characters leaning forward on their stools as they talked in lowered tones to the vendor looked pretty mean. But Mr. Mien was a businessman, he had to serve everyone who came to his stall; otherwise he might as well close shop. Yet, something was amiss. Suddenly, the men broke into rough, raucous laughter. One of them slapped his knee and the other bent back on his stool, his head thrown back, mouth open wide. Mr. Mien sat, bobbing his head, his lips parted in a half grin, and his hands rubbing the grease more thoroughly into the sides of his apron.

Before she could think anymore about the scene at the noodle stall, the street crowd started to move more quickly. Within seconds, a stately palanquin on the shoulders of four men came through the street. A column of servants preceded it and cleared the area of people, allowing the party to advance without incident.

The servants approached the carpenter's shop

and stopped in front of the door. A tall figure in a long black robe descended from the carrier. This must be the famous Imperial Doctor Lum!

She ran back into the shop to tell Mrs. Mu and Guei-lung the doctor had arrived. By the time Doctor Lum reached the shop door, Mrs. Mu, Guei-lung, and Mei-hua stood together, ready to greet him.

Doctor Lum, being professional in every way, did not appear to notice the simplicity of the shop and the room in which the carpenter lay. The doctor sat on a nearby three-legged stool, accepted a cup of fragrant tea, and talked to Mrs. Mu about her husband's condition before examining the patient himself. While drinking his tea he never once glanced at the patient, instead giving his full attention to his wife and her conversation. Mei-hua and Guei-lung stood silently nearby ready to be of assistance, if needed.

Shortly, Doctor Lum rose, took his stool, and went to sit near Mr. Mu. First, without touching the patient, he carefully studied the carpenter's face. Mr. Mu had awakened at the commotion of the doctor's entrance, but he couldn't speak. He barely had the power to keep his eyes open. Doctor Lum said nothing during his observations. Finally, he took the sick man's hand and held it for a long time while feeling his pulse.

Finishing his examination, he rose and walked into the outer room. Mrs. Mu, Mei-hua, and Guei-lung followed.

"Could I see the medicines he's been taking, Mrs. Mu?"

"I'm sorry, Doctor. The bell-doctor comes every day and brings only enough medicine to give him at that time. I don't believe there's any left," Mrs. Mu replied, her voice quivering.

"'Don't believe?'" he repeated after her. "Now don't be nervous Madam, but I must ask you to please check to be sure you have none. Not even a small amount. You say you were never told what the medicine consisted of. Therefore, if there's any left, anything at all, I'd like to have it." Doctor Lum spoke with a calm, authoritative assurance.

Mrs. Mu promptly bowed her way out of the room and back into their private backroom. In the quiet of the shop they could hear her moving bowls and containers around. No one spoke; the doctor seemed lost in thought and unaware of Mei-hua and Guei-lung's presence.

Soon, the carpenter's wife returned with a small envelope.

"This is all I found. There's not much left, a couple of granules in the corner of the paper folds. And I added the dregs left in the bottom of the cup he last used to take his medicine." With shaking hands she handed the envelope to Doctor Lum.

He solemnly took the paper from her. "Thank you, Madam. This will help me. I fear your husband is in great danger. Don't give him any medicines, *any*, that I haven't given my personal approval for. Do you understand?" He bent his head to gaze directly into the elderly woman's eyes. She nodded a vigorous agreement.

"I wish I had come earlier for it may already be too late. Be prepared. Your husband may die within the week!"

# CHAPTER 3

DOCTOR LUM'S ANNOUNCEMENT sent shivers through Mei-hua. He was one of the best practitioners in the country. Madam Wu had told her that he received the highest honors at the Imperial Medical College and that there were few, if any, physicians more capable. If he thought Mr. Mu was in mortal danger, he was. Mei-hua remained rooted, waiting to hear more. What came next was even more baffling than she expected.

Doctor Lum's rumbling voice broke the silence. "Mrs. Mu I must now ask you to leave the room while I speak to Zhang Mei-hua and Hsu Guei-lung." The carpenter's wife looked at him, eyes brimming with tears. However, she didn't say anything; she simply nodded and turned to step back into the kitchen.

"What about the guard, Doctor? Should he leave, too?" Guei-lung asked. "He could wait in the adjacent room, if you'd like."

They all three glanced momentarily at the young soldier standing a few steps away from Mei-hua. His face was calm and noncommittal. His normally dancing eyes betrayed no thought or emotion.

"No. I'm not concerned about the guard. As a soldier in the magistrate's troops, his integrity is beyond reproach." Doctor Lum turned his gaze back toward Mei-hua and Guei-lung. He began to speak to Mei-hua in a lowered voice.

"I understand you are a close friend of the carpenter and his wife."

Mei-hua nodded.

"Then I must warn you to watch over Mr. Mu very carefully. Don't let him take any more of the bell-doctor's medicine. Note everything he eats or drinks and tell me when I return. I'll be gone for two days on business, but will come again to see how he is doing when I return. In the meantime, make sure Mrs. Mu gives him these." Doctor Lum began writing a list of medicines out on a sheet of paper, giving instructions on how and when to administer the dosages.

"I trust you," he looked at Guei-lung, "will be able to get these for them," his tone implied the medicines were quite expensive for the likes of this hard-working family.

Guei-lung nodded. "Yes, we'll take care of everything needed. There's no problem."

"Good." Doctor Lum handed the list over to him. Before he left, he bent toward Mei-hua and, again lowering his voice, said: "Your father has been my good friend for many years. Magistrate Hsu, who is also a fellow classmate from our early days, told me of your family difficulties. I'm sure there will be a positive resolution to your father's problems."

At these words, tears threatened to well up in her eyes, but she managed to hold them back. Concern for her father and his struggle against the charge of government mismanagement and, therefore, of treason, was never far from her mind. If he was found guilty of the trumped-up charges, he and every member of the Zhang family would be executed for crimes against the Emperor and the country. The Emperor had no tolerance of any potential acts against him or his government. As he had proven in the past when dealing with others suspected of working against him, his vengeance would be swift and violent.

"Just remember," Doctor Lum continued, nodding his head slightly, "he has many friends who are all willing to help." With these words, he removed an envelope from his sleeve and handed it to her. A wax seal had been secured to its surface.

Mei-hua took it with both hands and held it so she could read the seal. It consisted of two words: "wind" and "grass." She caught her breath. Before sending her to the household of Master Hsu, her father had given her a tea colored jade amulet which read: *When the wind blows, the grass must bend.* It was the same amulet he and a circle of his friends wore as a sign of their friendship and loyalty to each other. He gave the amulet to her to wear the day he sent her away in order to protect her from his enemies. She stared up at the doctor.

He tapped the envelope. "If you should need me in an emergency, send a letter to me in this envelope. I will respond immediately." With that, Doctor Lum turned and strode from the room.

Mei-hua, holding the envelope in her hands, touched it to her chest. She pressed it against the jade amulet she always wore next to her skin. When her father had given the amulet to her, he said it would guide and protect her. It had already done so in many ways. Now she was beginning to realize that it also led to a network of trusted friends.

Feeling the jade's coolness, Mei-hua was overwhelmed with questions and a nugget of hope. She whispered to Guei-lung, "Do you suppose he's one of our fathers' circle? That he also has an amulet? See the words 'wind' and 'grass' are on this envelope."

Standing close to her, he replied in a barely audible voice: "There's a good chance of it. He said he went to school with father. And that's when our fathers and their closest classmates made a pact to always, at any time, come to each other's aid. I wonder if he wears the same tea colored jade amulet, inscribed with their motto, like the others do."

Before Mei-hua and Guei-lung could continue their discussion, Mrs. Mu joined them. Her shoulders slumped, her feet dragged slightly over the worn floor, and her eyes were red; she struggled to not cry in front of them.

"Doctor Lum thinks he's going to die. My Mr. Mu is going to leave me!" She put her hands over her face as if to hide the tears threatening to tumble down her cheeks.

"He's very concerned," Mei-hua said gently. She pushed back thoughts of her father and reached out to the old woman. She took Mrs. Mu's arm and led her to a nearby stool. "But I'm sure Mr. Mu will recover. The doctor gave us a list of medicines for him to take."

Guei-lung showed the despairing woman the paper with the prescription written out. "We'll send a servant to get this filled immediately. Then we can go over the list together for how much and when Mr. Mu should take them."

"Oh, it's so long! It'll cost a fortune!" Mrs. Mu's eyes widened with concern.

"Don't worry, Mrs. Mu. My family will take care of this. Don't concern yourself with these costs; just take care of your husband," Guei-lung hastened to assure her.

Mei-hua gave him a quick look filled with appreciation.

"And," Mei-hua turned back to Mrs. Mu, "Doctor Lum said not to give Mr. Mu any other medicines. None. Only these he prescribed himself. It's critical that we do exactly what he ordered."

Mrs. Mu shook her head as if in confusion. "Not give him any other medicines? But what should I tell the bell-doctor? He's been so diligent. Never missing a day. Always bringing just the right amount of medication."

"I'll take care of that," Guei-lung said. "I'll let him know his services are no longer necessary."

"And what about his reputation?" a voice from behind them demanded.

They all twirled around towards the unexpected new-comer. Mr. Mien stood near the door holding a hot bowl of noodles.

"Oh, Mr. Mien! How kind of you to come!" Mrs. Mu jumped up from her stool and hastened to the skinny, stooped figure. She took the bowl with both hands. "Thank you for bringing this to the house."

She turned to Mei-hua and Guei-lung. "He's been so kind during Mr. Mu's illness. No matter how busy he is at his noodle stand, he brings soup with his own hands to my husband." Again her eyes reddened and began welling up with tears.

"Now, now, Mrs. Mu," Mr. Mien said while holding his hands up in a self-depreciating movement, as if trying to stop her praise. He allowed himself a crooked, half smile. "You'd do the same for me, I'm sure."

Wiping his hands on the sides of his apron, he continued "Did I hear you say the good doctor I sent over to help your husband is to be dismissed?" His tiny, watery eyes slid from Mrs. Mu to Mei-hua. "Is that correct? You no longer want his services?"

Mrs. Mu, still holding the steaming bowl, bent toward him. Then, as if cajoling a child, hurriedly said, "What is to be done? Magistrate Hsu sent for Doctor Lum to examine Mr. Mu and Doctor Lum himself requested this change. It is not that I have lost confidence in the good local doctor." With this simple explanation, she put all the responsibility for the decision on the magistrate and his wishes.

Mei-hua grimaced. She understood Mrs. Mu's trying to smooth over any hard feelings with the noodle vendor. The elderly woman was in a fragile state. Her husband was critically ill and she desperately sought all the good-will she could muster from those in this world and in the nether world. Nevertheless, the noodle vendor made Mei-hua's skin crawl, and his repeated objections in favor of the local bell-doctor were making an already difficult situation even harder. It was only with Mrs. Mu's earlier admonition still ringing in her ears that she managed to maintain a silent and respectful stance.

"Ah, but you understand the problem, Mrs. Mu," Mr. Mien said. "If you dismiss the bell-doctor at this point, it will damage his reputation. He will lose business because people will lose confidence in him. All because of what another doctor says." His tone suggested Doctor Lum was no different than the bell-doctor, and implied Doctor Lum's request was professional jealousy.

"I am sorry, Mr. Mien," Guei-lung said, breaking into the conversation. "My father chose Doctor Lum. I will personally go over to the bell-doctor's house and thank him for all the help he has given Mr. Mu. But his services are no longer needed." Mei-hua was surprised at Guei-lung's authoritative, dismissive tone. She felt a surge of pride at his boldness in speaking to the noodle vendor in such a way.

Mr. Mien raised his eyes in surprise at Mrs. Mu. "Does this boy speak for you, Madam?"

"No offense is intended, Mr. Mien," Mei-hua interjected. "I'm sure we all appreciate what you've done to help your neighbor. But, as you can see, Mr. Mu has become significantly weaker; it is time for a change. Asking a second doctor to come onto such a difficult case is common. No one will think less of the bell-doctor. We'll see that no ill words are spoken about him."

Mei-hua was sure Mr. Mien was taking the change of doctors personally because he had recommended the local practitioner. The noodle stall owner had been a neighbor of the Mu's for a long time. She didn't want to offend him or to upset her kindly friend, Mrs. Mu, by developing a rift with her neighbor.

Again she reminded herself that, at a time like this, Mrs. Mu needed all the support she could get.

"Well, of course, nothing can be done now," Mr. Mien replied. "And," he looked directly at Mrs. Mu, "shall Mr. Mu no longer need to eat either? What about the nutritious pork and noodle soup?" he asked, inclining his head in the direction of the bowl she held in her hands.

Mrs. Mu gave a strained laugh. "Mr. Mien, as long as you're kind enough to sell this healthy soup, Mr. Mu will eat it. And with pleasure," she added.

Not entirely mollified, Mr. Mien gave slow inquiring looks at Mei-hua and Guei-lung.

"Doctor Lum did not specifically say Mr. Mu should not eat pork and noodle soup," Mei-hua replied to his look. She carefully kept her tone neutral, but it was difficult. "He must eat something."

This whole conversation irritated her. What right did this man have to put Mrs. Mu on the defensive? So what if he has had a stall outside the carpenter's door? His stall's location didn't give him special privileges. Besides, she didn't remember the couple ever speaking of him as a friend or even close associate in the past. Come to think of it, they had no history of friendship, as far as she knew. He was a neighbor. Yes. He was being kind to them during this current illness. Yes. Now she began to wonder: Was that enough reason for her to deny her own nagging doubts about him?

As her eyes followed Mrs. Mu to the carpenter's bedside and watched the bent, worn figure feed the soup to her husband, Mei-hua still debated with herself, as she lightly chewed on her left thumb. Was she being too critical? The noodle vendor was irritating and overly defensive, true, but to be fair—as her father always encouraged her to be—he'd also been helpful and supportive. Perhaps his own past suffering at the loss of his wife and son did make him more sensitive to the grief and pain of others. Why should she be so untrusting and suspicious of him? Another thing her father always told her was to follow her instincts. But how would she know if she was right? In this time of anxiety, the Mus needed every bit of support, whatever its source. Sometimes difficult times brought out real kindness in others. Softening, Mei-hua stopped chewing her finger and smoothed the top of her tunic. Finally, she turned to Mr. Mien again.

"We certainly recognize all you've done, sir. Your continued kindness to Mr. and Mrs. Mu is deeply appreciated." Mei-hua bowed. Following her example, Guei-lung murmured thank you and also bowed.

"Well, well," Mr. Mien said, slipping his hands over his hair and replying in a whiny voice. "You are too kind. I am simply doing what any neighbor would do."

Before any more half sincere "thank yous" and "you're welcomes" could be proffered back and forth, Mrs. Mu returned, leaving the partially eaten bowl near her husband's bedside.

"My child," she began talking to Mei-hua, "I've been thinking about what Doctor Lum said of Mr. Mu's condition." She spoke with resolve, but her eyes became red again, even as her face lost its color. Clearly, it was all she could do to keep the tears back. Mei-hua put a hand out to help her to the stool, but Mrs. Mu chose to remain standing.

"I think it's time to bring in Buddhist monks to say prayers and to petition for a longer life for Mr. Mu." Before Mei-hua could say anything, she continued. "The prayers will help Doctor Lum in his work of bringing my husband to good health."

Mrs. Mu would not say the word "die" out loud for to do so would bring bad luck, and maybe even death, to Mr. Mu. Using good luck words such as "long life" and "good health," however, would not hurt him and might even bestow on him the good health he lacked. Mei-hua was sure Mrs. Mu wanted the Buddhist priests' prayers to bring her husband a long life, but it was also a form of insurance. Mei-hua now realized that by wanting the Buddhist priests to be here also meant Mrs. Mu was aware of how sick her husband was. She was preparing for what seemed to be inevitable. If he should die within a few days, they would be here to make sure his soul traveled safely to the nether world.

"I've already sent one of the servants to get the medicines Doctor Lum ordered. Even so, I can leave for the Misty Temple right now," Guei-lung quickly volunteered, naming a famous Buddhist temple located just outside the city's walls.

"No, wait Guei-lung," Mei-hua countered. "We need to discuss this with your father first. He'll be upset if he learns we went so far by ourselves, especially outside the city gates." She hurried on so Guei-lung couldn't protest and, worse yet, demand she remain behind while he went to the temple without her. "Plus, to do the prayers properly we need several Buddhist monks and that will require the permission of Misty

Temple's Abbot. He is more likely to send a larger number of monks if your father requests it than if we request it by ourselves."

After a short pause, Guei-lung said, "You're right. We must tell Father all. But I'll still insist on taking the request to the temple myself!"

Mei-hua smiled at his determination to carry out this request for Mrs. Mu.

"Yes, of course. And I will join you." After a quick review of the minimum number of monks Mrs. Mu believed necessary for a healing ritual, the two returned to the Hsu household. Once again, Guei-lung and the young soldier led the way, causing the street crowds to part and allowing the palanquin to pass through without incident.

Since Guei-lung's mother was responsible for running the household, and Buddhist prayers for the sick were part of those duties, they immediately went in to speak with her. She would report to Master Hsu later. After hearing all they had to say, Madam Wu ordered the servants to bundle a large array of gifts for the temple: food, cloth, and bedding. After all was arranged, she put in a couple of silver bars. She told them how important it was to impress upon the Abbot the necessity of producing a top quality prayer session and, therefore, it was best to show the highest respect and concern for the temple and its monks. These gifts did just that. Besides, the religious generosity of the Hsu house was well known to the Abbot. Madam Wu regularly gave liberal offerings to the temple.

It took quite a bit of convincing to get her to allow Mei-hua to accompany Guei-lung on the trip to

Misty Temple. For, although women orchestrated much of the alms giving to the temples and to the monks, they rarely went personally to visit with the Abbots. When women did go to the temples, they stayed among themselves and usually only visited with women who had joined the religious life as nuns.

Nevertheless, in the end, the two young people were able to convince her Mei-hua would be safe traveling with Guei-lung, her personal guard, and the many servants needed to carry them and their offerings. After all, Madam Wu reasoned aloud, the Emperor's own soldiers protected the area, keeping thieves away. She firmly credited the personal involvement of Lord Chiu, the local commanding officer and the Emperor's most trusted eunuch, for the current safety of travelers. There had not been one highway robbery in over a year.

Within the hour, Madam Wu had everything in order and the palanquins ready to travel. Guei-lung rode in one while Mei-hua rode in another. The alms were boxed or placed in outsized baskets and hung from bamboo rods carried on the shoulders of a dozen servants.

Through a small opening in her palanquin's curtain, Mei-hua observed the young soldier moving among the servants. He made sure the boxes and baskets were secured and spoke to each servant, his voice low and unintelligible. At the end of his statements, however, each carrier nodded his head in response and hoisted the burden onto his shoulder, ready to go.

Without appearing overbearing or hurried, the young soldier managed to orchestrate the line of servants so that within a short time everyone was ready to move out. Mei-hua watched him as he loped past her palanquin, pausing to tell her carriers to get ready as he passed. His dimple showed even when he was serious. She liked that.

As she was thinking about Soldier Guo's dimple, her seat jerked awkwardly upward, causing her to fall against the side of the palanquin. A sharp pain shot through her upper arm. She grimaced. The carriers had just hoisted the palanquin up onto their shoulders, causing it to abruptly rock from side to side and front to back. Mei-hua hastily drew away from the window and settled down for the journey to Misty Temple.

Finally, she heard the young soldier give the order to proceed. The party made an impressive sight as they left the Hsu compound.

Although the temple was less than two miles from the city gates, they didn't have much time to waste if they were to bestow their alms, talk to the Abbot, and return with the monks before the city gates closed for the night. The entourage traveled as speedily as possible. In the city, their lead servant noisily cleared the way for them and they moved swiftly through the crowded streets by warning pedestrians the palanquins were coming. Once outside the city, however, the little parade traveled more quietly.

Mei-hua kept a bit of curtain pulled back, enabling her to peruse the countryside as they passed through it. She'd never been to the temple before and wasn't sure exactly where they were. She wished she and Guei-lung could travel together in one palanquin. They still needed to discuss more about what they would do and say at the temple. But she knew traveling together was impossible. Young unmarried men and women never spent time alone unchaperoned. To do so would be scandalous and ruin her reputation.

Eventually, she spotted a grove of ancient trees. Before they left, Guei-lung had told her about a stand of old oaks just outside the temple. They were famous for their age and represented long life, making them an auspicious symbol for those traveling by them. This was good, Mei-hua thought. The temple must be quite close.

The air cooled significantly and smelled sweeter as they arrived in the shadows of the soaring majestic trees. Pushing the curtains further apart, Mei-hua breathed the delicious air deeply into her lungs. How delightful! She closed her eyes to enjoy the sensation even more.

Just as she was thinking Mr. Mu would recover faster if he were able to breathe this fresh air instead of being closed up in the back of his shop, a loud yell and then more screaming voices startled her out of her reverie. Her palanquin rocked precipitously. She grabbed onto the window frames. The curtains swung about but still blocked her sight. She desperately wanted to look out, but couldn't release her grip or she'd be thrown about like a rag doll.

Even as the adrenalin pumped through her veins, panic rose like acrid bile in her throat. She frantically pushed against the palanquin's side to keep from crashing against the wooden walls and ceiling, then grabbed hold of the door handle to keep from being thrown into the opposite wall.

Suddenly she heard Guei-lung call out,

"Robbers!" followed by another shout to the carriers, "Stay together! Don't run away!"

# CHAPTER 4

MEI-HUA, WITH HER ADRENALIN PUMPING, flung open the door of the violently jostling carrier. With one last mighty push against the seat, she burst out into the open, dropping close to him.

At the same time, a scream of pain seared the air. Mei-hua swung around to see Guei-lung fall to the ground. Soldier Guo and three large servants quickly surrounded him, facing outward to fight off the onslaught of robbers.

Swiftly surveying the scene, Mei-hua saw the men who carried her palanquin crouching further away, hiding behind their bundles. Three other men, faces covered with large pieces of red cloth, appeared on the other side of her chair. They held their blades high as they approached the unarmed figures.

"Watch out!" Mei-hua yelled in warning. "They have knives!"

Instantly and instinctively, the martial arts lessons from her old servant overcame her rising panic. She bounded toward the carriers. When the frightened men saw her—a young woman rushing towards them with her silk coat flying behind her, arms raised to come to their defense—it gave them courage. They picked up their loads and thrust them forward with all their might, knocking the robbers over. The robbers leapt back onto their feet. Two had dropped their knives but came forward, fists ready. Then, before Mei-hua could reach the servants, one of the robbers whose face was wrapped in a dark cloth called out in muffled Mandarin, "Get out of here! Run! We're finished!"

The attack ended as quickly as it started. The robbers disappeared, as if by magic.

Mei-hua stared. Where did they go? Even in such a dense grove of trees she should have seen or heard something. What happened?

Then the silence was broken by the sound of running and a loud, rough voice giving orders. She caught sight of several men wearing military uniforms dashing through the trees. The local security forces had arrived. Trusting them to search out the robbers, Mei-hua turned back.

Before she had taken two steps, however, Soldier Guo ran up to her, eyes blazing.

"What were you doing? Why didn't you stay in the palanquin?" he demanded, his brows knit over dark flashing eyes.

In a flush of anger at being questioned, Mei-hua lashed back, "Where were you? You're supposed to be my guard! You tell me what happened!" Even as the words tumbled out of her mouth, Mei-hua knew she was being unfair. She had seen him protecting Guei-lung. Even so, she could not help herself from retaliating. Who did he think he was, demanding an explanation from her?

Standing in front of her, alternately clenching and releasing his grip on the spear which he had just moments ago wielded as a weapon, a look of frustration crossed his face. Then, bowing, he said, "Miss Zhang, I apologize for speaking out and neglecting my duty. Please forgive me." He kept his head down, not looking at her, waiting for a reply.

"Yes," Mei-hua said, growing warm with embarrassment. "We both spoke too quickly," she added, as a way of apologizing for her own outburst. "And what about Guei-lung? Is he all right?"

The young man raised his head and, turning towards the palanquins, answered, "Yes. He's fine. A slight wound, but no serious ...."

"Oh, he's wounded!" Mei-hua spun around and rushed to the knot of servants.

The men parted at her approach, revealing Guei-lung doubled-over on the ground. He was unusually pale and held his right arm at an odd angle.

"How is he?" she asked as she carefully stepped closer.

"It's his arm, Mistress. The robbers broke it in the attack." One of the carriers volunteered.

Before Mei-hua could enquire further, the rough voice she had heard moments earlier demanded, "What? The robbers attacked him? Was he protecting your boxes, then?" Mei looked away from Guei-lung just long enough to see that the voice belonged to a tall, robust man in an officer's uniform.

"No, sir. He was leaning out of this chair when one of the robbers, a giant of a fellow, hoisted him out by his arm and tried to stab him," the carrier said.

"Stabbed him!" Mei-hua repeated in alarm. "Where?" She moved to his side, searching for blood from a wound. No blood. She nodded to herself, satisfied that somehow the robber's knife missed. Still mystified, she turned back and asked, "Why would they yank him out of the chair and stab him?"

The officer glared at Mei-hua, a mere girl, asking questions and appearing much too bold in public. Then, as if she had not spoken at all, he asked, "Why? If they were robbers, why would they attack the young gentleman? Are you sure they just pulled him out without his having provoked them or ..."

"Yes, I'm sure. He didn't have time to do anything. He peeked out and this guy immediately grabbed him and pulled him to the ground. He might have been hurt bad if Soldier Guo hadn't come up as fast as he did."

Mei-hua pointed to their bundles the carriers had dropped. "But they didn't take the gifts we were bringing to the temple. Why would they attack Guei-lung instead of grabbing our gifts and making a rapid escape?"

The brawny officer again glared at Mei-hua. She suspected he thought she may be from a wealthy and, probably, powerful family, but her behavior proved she had poor upbringing. She should not be making a spectacle of herself in front of strange men by talking and asking questions.

Guei-lung interrupted with a groan.

"Oh! He needs to see a doctor right away," Mei-hua said.

Soldier Guo, who now stood near her, said, "He dislocated his elbow when they hauled him out of the chair and threw him on the ground. That's why his arm hangs at such an unnatural angle. Still, he's lucky he's not dead. See where the knife cut through his tunic. It's a miracle he wasn't killed. How the robber missed him, I'll never know," he continued as he knelt next to Mei-hua, inspecting Guei-lung for wounds. "Amazing that he wasn't even scratched by the robber's knife," he repeated.

Ignoring the officer's obvious disapproval of her speaking out, Mei-hua asked again: "Why do you think they would attack him when all they had to do was grab for the packages and run? We only had one guard." She paused and, looking directly at the officer, added, "Madam Wu didn't think we needed many guards since Lord Chiu, the Emperor's powerful eunuch, had cleared the bandits out of the area."

"Yes," the hulking officer replied, defensive at her implied criticism of his neglecting his duty. "The area can be cleared of ruffians, but who is to say when another gang may try out their luck on some hapless traveler?

"Besides," he continued looking steadily down at Guei-lung, "I'd say these men were not ordinary robbers."

"What do you mean," Mei-hua quickly shot back. "What else could they be?"

"Robbers are simple people," the officer scoffed and spit on the ground. "Not complicated at all. They want money or goods to sell. Simple," he repeated and paused. Glancing at the porters, their loads, and the palanquins, he scowled and continued, "And yet...Yes, why pull this young gentleman out of his chair? Why attempt to kill him when he wasn't a barrier between them and the loot?" He stopped again, frowning and leaving his question unanswered.

Mei-hua impatiently demanded, "All right, who were they, if not robbers?" She flung her arms out to encompass the whole scene. "Who else would do this kind of thing?"

"Well, I don't have any proof, but," he paused again, "if I were to hazard a guess, I'd say those men were secret society members."

Mei-hua stared at him, shocked. Large bands of criminals, often organized under the leadership of men who were the pillars of society, formed powerful and dangerous secret organizations. They kidnapped, committed extortion, and even murdered for hire or for their own inscrutable reasons.

The officer's eyes held Guei-lung's as he asked, "Do you know why someone might want to kill you?"

# CHAPTER 5

GUEI-LUNG GRIMANCED AT THE PAIN radiating from his right arm. He held it gingerly in his left hand as he tried to answer the officer's questions. Neither he nor Mei-hua could shed any light on the attack. A deliberate attempt on his life seemed all but preposterous. The only possible reason the officer could think of was Guei-lung's status as the magistrate's son. Although how this connected to the attack wasn't clear in any way.

"This must be reported to the authorities immediately. Both the magistrate and Lord Chiu," the officer said.

Mei-hua, frustrated by the delay in their mission to help Mr. Mu and now concerned for the health of yet another friend, declared that Guei-lung's injury was their first concern. They had to continue onto the Misty Temple where he could be treated. As with most large Buddhist temples, the monks living there also operated a hospital for the poor. With their medical expertise, they would be more than capable of setting his arm.

With Guei-lung suffering severe pain, it didn't take much to convince the officer to go on to the temple. The military escort safely brought them to its gates, then quickly returned to the city in order to speak to the magistrate and send a report on to the imperial eunuch.

Seeing the soldiers and numerous carriers arriving with the two ornately adorned palanquins, the Abbot sent his monks out to welcome the unexpected visitors.

Mei-hua descended first, causing a stir. Young women never traveled to temples alone and never presented themselves to the monks and Abbot without a chaperone. Although she realized how unseemly her behavior appeared, she remained undaunted by the cluster of monks who frowned at her, a lone female coming to their temple. She stood at the side of her palanquin next to her young guard. Giving Soldier Guo a swift, unobtrusive glance, she noticed his lean face had a slightly amused look. His brown eyes rimmed with black lashes once more seemed to light up with barely controlled laughter.

*Well, I'm glad he's amused*, she thought with annoyance. *This is an important mission and I have a guard who doesn't take anything seriously*. Trying to ignore him, Mei-hua continued to stand, waiting for someone from the temple to present himself to her—just as he would to any significant visitor.

After a few moments of confusion among the monks, one stepped forward and said, "Welcome to Misty Temple." He seemed uncertain as to what to say next.

"Thank you. I am honored to be here. Unfortunately on our way to the temple our group was attacked by bandits and one of our people has been wounded. His arm is broken and needs to be set," Mei-hua said.

At this, the monk said, "Please, let us tend to your injured party. We have an excellent infirmary here. Our hospital has been officially sanctioned by the government to care for the sick and injured. Your servants can follow the monks to the hospital grounds," he pointed to a smaller gate to the back of the main courtyard.

She nodded and directed Guei-lung's men to follow one of the monks. As they carried him to the hospital, she said, "It would be my honor, as a representative of Magistrate Hsu, to visit with Misty Temple's Abbot. Magistrate Hsu apologizes for not being able to come personally; he regrets that court business keeps him away. However, through his son Hsu Guei-lung and myself, he sends alms for the temple and hopes the Abbot will accept them as a small gesture of his respect." After this long-winded speech, she bowed and waited.

In spite of the unusual circumstances, the still flustered monk assured her the Abbot would be pleased to have an audience with her—as Magistrate Hsu's representative. Mei-hua couldn't fail to notice how he carefully added the last, so she would understand why an important person like the Abbot would meet with her, not only a woman but one who was almost a child. However, Mei-hua didn't have to wait long before being admitted into the Abbot's office.

The first thing she noticed when she walked into the room was the magnificent murals painted in brilliant, intense colors on each of the side walls. On one side were scenes depicting stories of the great Monkey King and his travels to bring back the Buddhist sutras.

Mei-hua had seen popular plays about his adventures and recognized the story immediately. But it was the second wall which instantly attracted her attention. It held two large scenes. The first showed the Queen Mother of the West picnicking in the Peaches of Immortality Garden; the second portrayed a group of figures known as the Eight Immortals clustered together in a boat crossing the Eastern Sea. Several of the gods wore rags and resembled beggars. Of these, two in particular stood out to her. The first wore only a single shoe and had one bare foot, yet he appeared carefree and cheerful, as if he were dancing. In one hand he carried a pair of long castanets and in the other a basket of flowers. The gaiety of his appearance was infectious, and she smiled as she let her gaze slide to the immortal standing next to him. Suddenly, she stopped mid-step, transfixed by the image of a cripple with a scraggly beard. He leaned heavily on a crutch and held a bottle gourd, a calabash. She trembled and stepped closer to the painting. Could it be? This looked exactly like the beggar they had seen in the street as they left the Hsu compound.

Mei-hua glanced around; Soldier Guo didn't seem to have noticed the picture or the resemblance to the street beggar. After a momentary pause, she recovered from her shock. Now wasn't the time to think about this. The Abbot was waiting.

She continued forward and greeted the Abbot with a deep bow. He sat cross-legged on an elevated platform. A thin man of an indecipherable age, he waved her forward. If he found it unusual to have a young woman bring such a large donation to his temple—with

only an injured gentleman and several servants in tow—
he did not indicate his astonishment in any way.

"Welcome to Misty Temple," he said in a clear, bell-like voice. His calm, gentle face spoke volumes to her. She instantly felt comfortable with him but she remained standing, as was proper.

"Come, sit and tell me about your trip. I understand you and your company ran into some trouble on the road." Naturally, the monks would have told him about their encounter with the bandits.

"This has been a very strange trip," she said, "although it ended well. For we are here and able to present Magistrate Hsu's gifts to the Temple."

"Were you able to identify the bandits?" the Abbot asked.

"None of our group recognized any of the attackers. They tied red pieces of cloth around their heads, covering their faces. I heard one fellow speak, but his voice was muffled. All I can say is that he spoke Mandarin, not a local dialect. I might be able to identify his voice if I hear it again. Although that seems unlikely," she added as an afterthought. She told him what little she could about the incident, answering a few of the questions he had. Finally, she sat quietly, eyes down, having finished telling her story.

The silence remained unbroken.

Mei-hua glanced up at the Abbot. She wondered if he had gone to sleep. When she looked up she was captured by his penetrating gaze.

"Tell me about the Eight Immortals," he said.

She didn't know what to say. *What does he mean?* she wondered but didn't dare voice her confusion.

"You recognized something when you saw the mural of the Eight Immortals as you came into the room. Tell me about it." The tone of his voice was inviting, not commanding. Yet, she knew she couldn't refuse.

"I ... This may sound strange," she began.

"Nothing is strange when it comes to the Immortals," he said.

Mei-hua nodded. "It's just that I'm sure I saw one of them on the street." She shook her head. "But that's not possible."

His silence opened the door for her to continue.

"We were leaving the compound to visit a sick friend when a vagrant came up to us and said: 'What is true may seem false and what is false may seem true. Look into your heart to find the truth. However, if you don't recognize the truth, death will result.'" She was surprised by how easily she remembered his words. After a moment, she added, "But he was probably just a beggar and was simply babbling."

"And, you think he looked like the Immortal with the crutch?" he asked, ignoring her last comment.

"Yes," she admitted again because the resemblance was so unsettling. "He looked just like the Immortal standing in the middle of the boat."

"That's Iron-crutch Li." The Abbot folded his hands together in his lap. "Often people only think of the Eight Immortals as representing prosperity and longevity. Those are important, of course. However, they also love justice and fight evil. It very well may be that Iron-crutch Li was warning you. You must take his words seriously. The Immortals would not deceive you on such a matter." He leaned forward and pressed his fingers together. "If the Eight Immortals have chosen to help you, it's more than possible that you will encounter Iron-crutch Li or another of the Immortals again. When you need them, of course."

A shutter ran down her spine. An image of her friends, the carpenter and his wife, flashed through her mind. She looked down, a sense of foreboding filling her. What would she need protection from?

He asked questions and listened carefully and fully to the answers. Mei-hua sensed he was another man of Magistrate Hsu and her father's quality, a man of knowledge and wisdom who cared about people and sought to do what was best.

After a few more comments about the attack, Guei-lung's condition, and Iron-crutch Li, she finished by again relaying Magistrate Hsu and Madam Wu's greetings. He already knew she had brought many packages and boxes as alms for the temple, but she restated they were gifts from the Hsu household. Then, as if it would be a favor he granted to the magistrate and Madam Wu, she asked him to dispense a contingent of monks to the carpenter's house to pray for Mr. Mu's longevity.

She told him of the carpenter's illness and how, although Doctor Lum had started to treat him, Mrs. Mu wanted to improve his chances to get well by having the monks pray for him.

"Naturally, Magistrate Hsu and Madam Wu will gladly pay any additional costs the temple incurs for Mr. Mu's benefit."

He waved a hand. "Not to worry. All will be taken care of." He turned toward the monk who had brought her to him and said, "Have four of our brethren prepare for a multi-day vigil. They should leave as soon as possible for the carpenter's home."

The monk bowed and glided out of the room as smoothly as a panther.

"Thank you so much, Honorable Sir," Mei-hua said gratefully. As she watched the monk leave to fulfill the Abbot's orders, a burden lifted from her heart. The arrival of the monks at the carpenter's home would bring tremendous comfort to Mrs. Mu. Hopefully their presence and prayers would also strengthen Mr. Mu as he lay in such a dire state.

The Abbot scrutinized Mei-hua. The slight slump of her shoulders told of her exhaustion. The stress of the trip out to the temple, not to mention the events of the day, had been trying.

"You must stay here for a rest. The nun's quarters has a guest room. It is simple, but adequate. You can share a vegetarian meal with the nuns, during which they can also enlighten you concerning the Buddhist sutras. In the meantime, the monks will continue treating your companion. If all goes as expected, he can return home with you."

While he was talking, a flutter of saffron near the door caught her eye. A novice had entered the audience hall. He slipped noiselessly to the Abbot's side and whispered to him.

Mei-hua watched. Although his voice was barely audible, she thought she heard Guei-lung's name mentioned. She hoped the novice was reporting on his condition.

When the young man stepped back, the Abbot said, "Hsu Guei-lung is doing fine. His arm had been yanked out of its socket, as you thought. The monks are in the process of setting and restraining his arm, allowing it to heal properly."

The Abbot's melodious voice went on, "The monks are leaving the temple at this time. They will soon set up at the carpenter's home and begin their prayers to intercede for Mr. Mu's soul and postpone his passing on to the afterlife. Given the gravity of his condition, I didn't want the monks to wait for your return."

He leaned toward her. "I'm sure that, while you're deeply concerned about Hsu Guei-lung, you also want the monks to begin their prayers as soon as possible," he said.

She nodded.

"Yes. Now you don't have to worry about that. And, as I have said, you may take Guei-lung home with you later today. I know his parents well; they will need to follow-up with another doctor to make sure no complications develop. Otherwise, all is well."

He waved a hand toward the window. They could hear monks calling back and forth as they prepared to leave.

"Thank you. I will do as you say," Mei-hua said. She was, in fact, delighted with this plan. She was exhausted, and she was also keenly aware of the problems facing her once they returned to the Hsu compound. Madam Wu especially would be upset by their run-in with bandits and her son's injury. Without a doubt, she would blame herself for allowing them to travel to the temple. Mei-hua was almost certain Madam Wu, taking her role as Mei-hua's surrogate mother seriously, would not allow her to go out of the compound again for fear that she, too, would be hurt. She only hoped that when his mother saw he had already been treated and was otherwise in good health, her concern would be somewhat mollified.

Plus, she reasoned, having Guei-lung under her care would give his mother a mission and hopefully divert her attention and anxiety. He was better off at home, anyway. After all, the Abbot was right: the Hsu family could provide better care than any public hospital. Those hospitals were not meant to treat people who could afford their own care. In fact, she was sure his being in the hospital for more than a day would shame his family.

After the Abbot gave her a short blessing, Mei-hua was taken to the nun's quarters. Their rooms had none of the brilliant tile work found in the main part of the temple and in the Abbot's area; these rooms were stark in their simplicity with only a few sutras hanging on the red brick walls. Nevertheless, the nuns' warm welcome seemed to cast a glow over the rooms.

Although they urged her to take a nap to refresh herself, she was too restless and too concerned about getting Guei-lung back to the city before the gates closed at dark. Finally, after what seemed forever, a messenger came into the quarters to report on Guei-lung. He was ready to travel.

Mei-hua didn't worry as much about being attacked on the trip back because there were no burdens weighing down the poles the carriers balanced on their shoulders. Now they merely hung with swaying empty baskets and could easily become weapons for protection. Soldier Guo and all of the men walked with heightened awareness; there would be no surprise attack.

Jostling on the shoulders of four servants, curtain closed, Mei-hua sat in the palanquin's dimmed interior. Tension radiated through her back and neck. Her entourage was ready, but it didn't stop her from brooding about what was behind the earlier attack. Swaying back and forth, she reviewed what had happened today.

The officer seemed quite certain the attackers weren't ordinary bandits. His suggestion about their being members of a secret society bothered her. How could their little group have been the specific target of an organized crime gang? They had just decided to come to the Misty Temple this morning after Doctor Lum's visit. The attack had to be random.

True, the bandits had not been active in this area outside the city for some time. However, did that mean they should jump to the conclusion their party was an intentional target of secret society activity? It didn't make sense. It's not as if Guei-lung made frequent and routine visits to the temple. In fact, she'd understood that this was the first time in five years he'd come. And then, she was an even more unlikely target. She had never been there before.

As she sat wrapped in thought, the trip back passed quickly for Mei-hua. Before she knew it, they had entered the city gates and were almost home. Hearing familiar sounds, she peeked around the heavy curtains. The noise and activity came from a neighborhood temple as workers set up for a fair scheduled to begin in two days. Many things had to be done in preparation. Several men worked on building a large stage for plays. A smaller stage for puppets would be set up tomorrow. Vendors and booths would soon appear along the roadway. They'd sell everything from food and candy to toys and clothing to sacred books, papers, and incense.

No sooner had she spied Mr. Mu's house, when Mr. Mien, the noodle stall owner, came out and spoke to a disheveled looking man. Then, catching a glimpse of Mei-hua and Guei-lung's approaching palanquins, the stranger left. Mr. Mien stood in the street, waiting for their arrival. When Mei-hua stepped out onto the road, he came up and, nervously rubbing one hand on the side of his apron, bowed slightly.

"Young mistress," he whined, "there's something of great importance I would like to speak to you about."

"Please excuse me. I'll be right back," she assured him as she kept walking toward the shop door. "Guei-lung's been hurt and I am taking him home. I must see Mrs. Mu before we..."

"This is most important, Miss," he moved in front of her, preventing her from entering the carpenter's shop.

Before Mei-hua could protest, however, Soldier Guo, who had been right behind her, stepped forward to remove him.

"Ah, ah, Miss," the noodle vendor sputtered, eyes darting back and forth between Mei-hua and her young guard. "I don't mean any harm. But I've important," he stressed the word as he repeated it, "*important* news."

Even though irritated by his obsequious manner, Mei-hua signaled for Soldier Guo to back away. She was beginning to like having the young guard around, at least when he was not laughing at her. Now, however, she paused. "Yes, of course. What's the problem, Sir?"

"The monks you sent from the Misty Temple ..."

"Yes. Good, they've arrived," she said. The sounds of strangers' voices came out from the house. She hoped it was the monks readying for their prayers.

"They've come! That's what I must tell you about! I know the head monk's assistant: he is a dangerous thief! His name is Da-shan!"

The news stunned Mei-hua. Da-shan! Images of the past raced across her mind's eye. He was a friend of her former kidnappers. He had tried to kidnap her himself when she was working for Mr. Mu. And now he is here inside the carpenter's house!

# CHAPTER 6

"I REMEMBER you mentioning him, Mei-hua," Guei-lung said as he approached while carefully cradling his injured arm in his left hand. "Isn't he the giant of a thief who threatened you before you joined our family?"

"Yes," she paused, "possibly." But, she was thinking, *How is this possible? How could a ruffian like Da-shan have infiltrated the Buddhist temple? For what purpose? Was he a member of the secret society's gang?*

"What makes you think it's Da-shan? How do you know him?" she asked the bony fellow in front of her."Having a noodle stand on the street, I meet many kinds of people and know a lot more about the low life in this part of the city than most good people might. I've seen this Da-shan a few times before. He has a bad reputation." Mr. Mien smiled his crooked, self-depreciating smile, "Naturally, I never have anything to do with him myself. I stay out of the way of the likes of him. But," he continued," I'm a poor tradesman, and I must know who the ruffians are to protect myself. You understand," he said avoiding Mei-hua and looking at Guei-lung while nodding his head in agreement with himself.

Guei-lung nodded back. "Certainly, a cautious man in business must be aware of the local dangerous elements. It's only right."

"But why would he be here, Mr. Mien?" Mei-hua asked again.

"Why that is simplicity itself!" he exclaimed. "He's here to discover where Mr. Mu keeps his valuables. Then, under the guise of praying for his health and well-being, Da-shan will be able to steal everything and anything. Who would suspect a monk? Undoubtedly he'll lay the blame on others."

Mei-hua glanced at Guei-lung, who was continuing to nod in agreement with Mr. Mien's analysis. She shook her head. "This may well be, but it seems like quite a complicated scheme for such a simple street thief."

"Never underestimate the man on the bottom!" Mr. Mien admonished. "Just because a man's uneducated and lives a rough and inelegant life doesn't mean that he isn't clever and capable of creating and carrying out well-designed crimes."

Mei-hua, taken aback by the emotion in Mr. Mien's speech, realized she'd offended him—again—and this diatribe referred to more than the thief. She hastened to pacify him, "I didn't mean to suggest the average person isn't intelligent. I only meant this particular plan of going around as a temple monk, on the chance you'll find a house with something to steal, is too full of "ifs" and happenstance. And then, even if he were successful, he would have to take the stolen goods back to the temple and hide them, so the other monks he lives with won't find out about them. This seems like an unlikely scenario for a man who had, up until now, been a common street thief."

"There is only one thing to do," Guei-lung interjected.

"You're right. We'll go in and talk to the man Mr. Mien claims is Da-shan," Mei-hua replied, completing his thought before he could finish it himself.

He nodded and added, "Don't worry. I'll talk to him."

She smiled. Guei-lung was always trying to be her protector. She allowed her glance to quickly take in Soldier Guo. Two protectors. But protecting her from what? With a barely perceptible shake of her head, she dismissed the notion she even needed protecting. Besides—she again slid a sidelong glance at Guei-lung and soldier Guo with a familiar thought—that these two were unlikely looking protectors. Her own past experience proved she had learned enough martial arts from her childhood servant, Old Lin, to allow her to take care of herself. *After all, in the end, don't we only have ourselves to rely on?* she thought.

*But, then again,* and here she smiled once more at Guei-lung, *if Guei-lung wanted to think he was defending me from something, why not let him?* And, with a quick glance at the young soldier, she was aware there was little she could do about Soldier Guo, since Magistrate Hsu himself had assigned him to her. At least having them around would not cause problems, and might come in handy in the future. Just as Soldier Guo proved here with the grungy old Mr. Mien.

Such were Mei-hua's thoughts as they entered the carpenter's small shop. She noticed the room had changed considerably since they left only hours ago. A chanting row of monks sat along one side of the room with religious paraphernalia spread in front of them. A large man, head bent over his joined hands, stood out.

Guei-lung went towards him, dropped respectfully to his knees and, holding his injured arm close to his body, carefully crawled close enough to speak softly to him. He didn't want to disturb the prayers of the other monks.

The monk reacted immediately to Guei-lung's whispering. His head jerked up and he stared at Mei-hua. A few hurried words passed between him and Guei-lung before he stood. Guei-lung remained in a lowered posture before the other chanting monks. The two men came over to her and Mr. Mien. The monk walked with his arms crossed in front of his chest and his hands hidden in his sleeves, but his face betrayed a sense of excitement.

Mei-hua realized Mr. Mien was right about the giant as soon as she saw him. This monk had to be Da-shan, her erstwhile kidnapper. She involuntarily took a step back as he approached.

When he reached her, however, he bowed low, saying, "Young mistress, do you recognize me? I am Da-shan. I never believed we would meet again in this world." He bowed deeply once more. "Since I last saw you, my life has changed and I have taken on the saffron robe of a monk. My life is dedicated to a search for enlightenment."

She didn't know what to think. Was it possible for a man to change so much in such a short amount of time? Her eyes flew from his face to Guei-lung's, who reflected her own amazement at this turn of events.

Soon, Mei-hua and Guei-lung extracted Da-shan's story and what happened to him since he'd attempted to abduct her. He claimed he developed a deep shame at being out-done by a mere girl. In his depression, he went to a tavern to drink his embarrassment away. On leaving the tavern, after getting as drunk as his money would allow, he ran into a ragged cripple leaning on an iron crutch. Without knowing why, an over-powering urge to tell the cripple about his experience made him stop and he blurted out his story. When he recounted the incident concerning Mei-hua and how she had overcome him and escaped his grip, the old tramp laughed. Da-shan was furious. However, the cripple explained that naturally she won, because clearly she, a mere girl, had used magic against him. How else could such a thing have happened? And, just as clearly, it meant the gods had turned against him. His life as a thief would never be the same. This was a sign for him to repent for all the wrong he had done in the past and give his life over to searching for the Way. He must take on the saffron robes, become a monk at the Misty Temple, and spend his life praying and begging for food.

Both Mei-hua and Guei-lung were amazed at his story. Nevertheless, his sincerity impressed them both, and they believed him.

Mr. Mien snorted and shook his head. "Bah! Since when does a man such as you truly give up the easy life of crime for the self-denial of a monk?" He spat on the floor. His spittle just missing Da-shan's sandaled feet.

"It is true, I swear," Da-shan began.

Cutting off the big man's protestations, the noodle vendor said, "I can prove you're using your monk's garb as a front for stealing."

Before Da-shan could protest, Mr. Mien continued. "Instead of coming directly into this house and preparing it for prayers, you had the monks come over to my stall on the pretense of begging for food before you began. Didn't you?"

Da-shan looked stricken. "Yes, we did seek alms before setting up in the house. But ..." he turned to Mei-hua and Guei-lung with a guilty face, trying to explain. "But ... Well, I know I should have had the monks come in immediately, but it was a long walk here, and we're going to be praying for the rest of the day and all night without a stop. How could it hurt to have a little food before we started?" He spread his hands out asking for understanding at his weakness of thinking of his stomach instead of concentrating on the well-being of the sick man. "As monks we can ask for alms. We're not supposed to pay for the food we eat."

Looking at Mr. Mien he added, "We did not steal from you. You freely gave each of us a bowl of soup. For that, you win merit for your soul. That is your reward, not money. So why are you accusing me of stealing?"

"Ah-ha. I'm not accusing your monks of stealing the soup, I'm accusing you, Da-shan, of stealing money from my little stall!"

At these words, Da-shan's face grew dark with anger. "What are you saying?" His voice rose into an ominous roar. Suddenly, the room fell quiet as the constant murmur of prayers that had filled the air abruptly stopped. Mei-hua shot a fleeting glance at the sitting monks. They were all staring at Da-shan. He turned toward his fellow monks and nodded for them to continue the prayers. The chanting resumed. Da-shan struggled to regain his temper.

Guei-lung spoke up. "Mr. Mien, what you're saying is a serious charge. What proof do you have that this man took your money? After all, your stall is out in the open on the street. If you're missing money, any number of people could have taken it while you were busy, or even while you were in here with Mr. Mu."

"My proof's an eye-witness, another customer of mine. He saw this man," Mr. Mien pointed dramatically at Da-shan, "slip behind the stall while I tended to the other monks' needs. He saw him take my money." He stressed the word *saw*, making it irrefutable evidence. "Now this thief is in here and we will probably find some of Mr. Mu's things missing, too!"

# CHAPTER 7

"A THIEF IN MY HOUSE! What's this! Wife, help me! Don't let ..." Mr. Mien's loud, blustery voice had wrenched the carpenter from his fitful sleep.

Mr. Mu's cries were cut off by a thump. His wife rushed toward the backroom.

"Come, help me!" she cried. "He's fallen!"

They all dashed forward, Soldier Guo ahead of them all. He quickly and carefully picked up the moaning carpenter. While Soldier Guo eased him back onto the bed, another figure entered the room, standing quietly near the door.

Mei-hua, thinking that it was a customer, stepped over to him. "I'm sorry, Sir, but as you can see Mr. Mu is not well at this time. May I help you?" As she finished her question, Mrs. Mu looked over and saw the man.

"Oh, Sir, you came just in time. Mr. Mu tried to get up and fell. Can you help us?"

Both Mrs. Mu's familiarity with the stranger and her asking him to help surprised Mei-hua. However, her questions were quickly answered.

"Doctor, I'm so glad you came," Mr. Mien exclaimed, pulling the man toward the sick bed as he spoke. "Mr. Mu appears to have collapsed. What should we do?"

Immediately, Mei-hua realized this newcomer must be the bell-doctor who had been tending to Mr. Mu. The very practitioner Doctor Lum ordered her to keep away from the sick man.

Moving between the local practitioner and the bed, Mei-hua bowed and said, "Sir, you don't need to trouble yourself about this incident. We've already sent for Doctor Lum." At this, she glanced quickly at Guei-lung, hoping he would understand her meaning.

"Yes, one of my servants went to his house. We will hear shortly," Guei-lung added smoothly, following her lead.

"But," Mrs. Mu, who was beside herself with grief, interrupted, "the good doctor is here. Why shouldn't he help Mr. Mu? It may take Doctor Lum hours to get here. What if he's not home, or is unable to come because of another appointment? Mr. Mu cannot wait. This good doctor has been treating him and knows him well."

Every time Mrs. Mu called the practitioner "good doctor" Mei-hua wanted to cringe. She wasn't going to be able to stop his working with the carpenter right now. She had no proof he hadn't done everything possible to help Mrs. Mu's husband in the past. And then there was the small problem that Doctor Lum had not really been sent for yet. Her claiming he had been called was simply a ruse to get this fellow out of the house. The imperial doctor wasn't going to turn up at any moment to help her sick friend. Having no other choice, Mei-hua stepped back and let the local doctor pass. She remained near, however, watching every move he made. She wanted to give Doctor Lum an accurate report later. At the same time, she again caught Guei-lung's eye and barely nodded her head toward him. She wanted him to send someone immediately for Doctor Lum.

Guei-lung nodded back and left the room. She knew he had understood. There were times when they seemed to be able to understand each other's thoughts.

Sensing eyes on her, Mei-hua turned. Soldier Guo stood to the side, watching them. *Of course,* she thought, *that's his job, to keep an eye on me.* Still, his scrutiny made her uncomfortable.

Guei-lung left the room to speak to his servants, and Mei-hua again shifted her gaze toward Soldier Guo. His lean, sensitive face appeared thoughtful as his eyes followed Guei-lung out the door. Then, he shifted and stared back at her. As he caught her gaze and held it with his own, the twinkle returned to his eyes and a smile tugged at the corners of his mouth.

Mei-hua was as irritated by this change of demeanor as by his intense scrutiny. *What did he find so amusing,* Mei-hua thought? *He is the worst example of a soldier I've ever seen.* Soldiers weren't supposed to stand around being amused while on assignment. Nevertheless, when she broke eye contact with him and turned away, she couldn't deny the unexpected surge of pleasure suddenly filling her chest.

The happiness only lasted an instant, however. Mr. Mu's silent figure stretched out on the bed with the practitioner nearby reminded her of the seriousness of the situation and of her responsibility.

In one slow, smooth motion, the bell-doctor

bent over the sick man, felt his wrist, put a hand on his chest, and turned to Mrs. Mu.

"Ma'am, I am sorry to tell you, your husband has just had a terrible shock, making his condition worse. There is nothing to be done to keep him in this world any longer."

"Oh, please, you must do something," Mrs. Mu pleaded. Mei-hua held her arm, supporting the despairing woman.

"Well," as if absorbed in thought, the bell-doctor studied his patient, "I do have a tonic, which could give him a chance to live. But I can't guarantee it will work. And it's quite expensive."

"Wait," Mei-hua quickly interjected before Mrs. Mu could respond. "Doctor Lum has tended to him, given him what he needs, and ordered that no other medicine should be administered. If we give Mr. Mu your new medicine, it might kill him." As she said this, she heard Mrs. Mu give a low groan of anguish.

"Mei-hua, do you think you know more about medicine than the good doctor, here? If he says Mr. Mu needs a special tonic, I think we must trust him to know what's best." Mr. Mien's whining voice broke into the conversation.

"I only have the patient's well-being in mind," the bell-doctor said, bowing politely toward Mrs. Mu. "Naturally, it is up to you, his wife, whether you wish to save him from death or not."

Furious, Mei-hua spoke sharply. "Mr. Mu is under the imperial doctor's care and should not take any other medicines right now. That is the best way 'to save him from death,' as you say."

Mr. Mien's eyebrows shot up. "Does this child speak for you, Mrs. Mu? Are you prepared to let your husband die because she doesn't want him to get proper care?"

"It's all right, Mr. Mien," the bell-doctor said. He thrust both hands up, palms out as if to stop the argument between the noodle vendor and Mei-hua. "Perhaps the young mistress is right. Doctor Lum is an important, knowledgeable doctor of the state. I would never want to go against anything he says to do," he said with a sympathetic shake of his head. He again turned towards the bent figure of Mrs. Mu, still supported by Mei-hua's arm. "If you prefer, I will leave a milder tonic with you. It will ease your husband's last moments. Naturally, all choices are up to you whether to use it or not. I will not give him the powerful rejuvenating medicine out of deference to you and your young friend here." Without waiting for a reply he again solemnly bowed and, glancing coldly at Mei-hua, started to prepare the medicine.

"Mrs. Mu, please use the local doctor's services while you still can," the noodle vendor urged. "You and your husband have been my neighbors for many years; I should hate to see him die now. Doctor Lum is not here and does not know of the great shock the thief, Da-shan, caused your husband. Certainly, if he were here, he would tell you to follow the bell-doctor's advice and save your husband's life."

Mrs. Mu straightened up. "I must do whatever is possible to save him. If Doctor Lum comes soon, I will follow his orders. Right now, I have no choice but to do as you say."

Mei-hua had to think quickly and change tactics to maintain control of the situation and to protect her friend until Doctor Lum arrived.

"If you wish for him to take these medicines, Mrs. Mu," Mei-hua said in a conciliatory voice, "I will give him the drink myself."

Mr. Mien and the bell-doctor both bobbed their heads in agreement. The smirk on the noodle vendor's face as the practitioner gave instructions on how to give the medicines to Mr. Mu wasn't lost on Mei-hua. Finally, the bell-doctor admonished her to make sure he drank the entire tonic. He was also to remain quiet with no noise to disturb him so that he could rest.

Mei-hua remained with Mr. Mu while Mrs. Mu followed the two men as they left the building. On the pretext of wanting to know why Guei-lung hadn't returned yet, Mei-hua told Soldier Guo to go out and try to discover what happened to him.

Left alone in the sick man's room, Mei-hua poured the tonic out in an old pot standing in a corner. She dripped the remaining few drops of medicine into one of Mrs. Mu's small containers and slipped it into her sleeves. She would give it to Doctor Lum to examine. Returning to Mr. Mu's side with the empty bowl, she heard loud voices from the front of the store.

"Arrest this man!" the noodle vendor's called out.

"What'd you mean?" She heard Da-shan shout back.

"Don't let him get away, Officer. He's a dangerous man."

Mei-hua flew to the door. She saw a uniformed

man holding tightly to Da-shan. Guei-lung, Soldier Guo, and the others encircled the officer and hapless monk.

"What's happening? Why is this man being arrested?" Mei-hua demanded.

"Theft and malicious harm to another," the officer replied.

"He has to be punished for stealing my money," Mr. Mien whined with indignation.

"What's the 'malicious harm to another'?" Mei-hua asked.

"Why, he's the cause of Mr. Mu's turn for the worse! Now he'll probably die," the noodle vendor said. As these unlucky words spilled out, Mrs. Mu's face whitened.

"How did he hurt Mr. Mu? He's been out here praying all this time," Mei-hua countered.

"Yes. He appears to be praying. But what prayers? To save my neighbor? No. Ask yourself: what is he really doing? If Mr. Mu doesn't get well, he can remain here—unnoticed, praying ..."

Mei-hua gave him a blank look. *What was this about?*

"... and take his time robbing the shop and house." The noodle vendor shook his head in exasperation at her lack of understanding. "He's been saying the wrong prayers to make his condition worse! How else do you explain Mr. Mu collapsing just as this thieving monk starts the praying? You said yourself Doctor Lum was here and treated Mr. Mu. It stands to reason the carpenter should be getting better, not worse. Only the powers of the supernatural could have overcome the care of an imperial doctor."

Pale and saddened, Mrs. Mu nodded in agreement to these words.

Stunned, Mei-hua stood rooted to the spot. She believed Da-shan when he said he'd become a monk to seek peace and enlightenment. She was sure he wasn't guilty of stealing. But how could she fight a charge of supernatural interference?

# CHAPTER 8

CERTAIN NO ONE WOULD GIVE Mr. Mu any more medicine, and with Mrs. Mu and the noodle vendor believing Da-shan was guilty of multiple crimes, Mei-hua realized she must talk to Magistrate Hsu. Once arrested, only the magistrate had the authority to protect the giant from being tortured by the jail's prison guards.

She sighed. Anyone arrested was assumed guilty, and torture usually guaranteed a full confession by even the most difficult criminal. Mei-hua closed her eyes. Even the truly innocent could end up with broken bones and other severe injuries. It was a brutal system, and she hoped to save Da-shan from it. Mei-hua had to return to the Hsu compound, promising Mrs. Mu she'd be back as soon as possible. What she didn't tell Mrs. Mu and the others was that she wanted to talk to the noodle vendor's customer who claimed to see Da-shan steal the money. Apparently, from Mr. Mien's description, the eyewitness was one of the men she'd often noticed at his stall.

She walked outside the shop with her shadow, as she now thought of Soldier Guo. Her palanquin stood ready for her. Before entering, she thoughtfully surveyed the people filling the street. A skinny man wearing the balloon pants and short white jacket of a laborer sat on one of the noodle vendor's stools. She was in luck; this was the fellow she wanted to see.

She called out to the gaunt figure. "Hey there."

Turning and seeing Mei-hua approach with a soldier behind her, he blanched. His eyes darted around as if looking for a place to hide.

"There's no problem," Mei-hua quickly assured him. "We," she said, including Soldier Guo, "want to talk to you for a second."

He stared at Soldier Guo, then tore his eyes away from him to give her a once over. Apparently unimpressed by what he saw, he demanded, "What're you doing here, little girl? Go home and leave me alone. I'm a simple working man and I don't need trouble from the likes of you." Although his words sounded tough, the tenor of his voice simply added to his nervous appearance.

"Please forgive my forwardness, Sir," Mei-hua said. "Are you the man who said he saw Da-shan loitering around the noodle stand?"

He stuffed his hands into his jacket's wide sleeves. "That's me."

"Could you tell us what you saw?"

With a quick glance at Soldier Guo, he said, "I work in the area, get odd jobs, and I often eat here. Today, while having lunch, I saw the guy they call Da-shan come up and wander around. He wore those orange robes, so naturally I thought he was a monk. Mr. Mien wasn't there. Da-shan seemed to be waiting for him to return and give him a bowl of noodles as alms."

He paused, licked his lips and looked away.

"What happened then?"

"You're not the court, why are you questioning me? Why should I talk to you?" He again retreated behind a barrage of hostile words.

"Would you rather talk to the court? We could help you out, if you do." Mei-hua began to gesture toward Soldier Guo.

"No. No. Don't misunderstand me. No problem," he hastily said, hands flying outward as if to stop her.

Mei-hua waited.

After fleetingly surveying the people milling about, he continued, "As I told the noodle vendor earlier, the monk walked around the stall and took some money out of a box Mr. Mien keeps under the table."

"Did you say anything to him?"

He cast a beleaguered glance at her, "I thought he was a monk. Mr. Mien is a pious man and could have told him to take the money as alms. What do I know? I'm just a poor, honest worker," he whimpered.

Mei-hua bowed. "Thank you for your cooperation, Sir. You have been most helpful."

When she stepped away and back toward her palanquin, she noticed Soldier Guo's dimple had deepened and his eyes gleamed with amusement.

Alone again in the gently rocking carrier, Mei-hua found the tangle of events disturbing. What was going on? So many problems seemed to be appearing at the same time the Mus had to deal with the carpenter's illness. She wondered if Guei-lung had been able to reach Doctor Lum. Touching the two small bottles with the remains of the practitioner's medicines, she also wondered what Doctor Lum would find when he examined them.

Entering the Hsu complex, the palanquin's carriers took her directly to the women's quarters. Unless they were relatives, men rarely came into the women's area. Therefore, Soldier Guo remained behind in the main section of the house, unable to follow her. As she descended from the carrier in the courtyard, she spied Madam Wu standing on the veranda, watching her.

Mei-hua immediately went up to the matriarch and bowed in greeting. Madam Wu waved her bow aside and told Mei-hua to come along with her and eat after such a long day. However, Mei-hua insisted she needed to talk to Master Hsu first. To placate the concerned matriarch, Mei-hua assured her she would share supper with her and Ping-an later.

Somewhat mollified, Madam Wu dispatched one of the maids to Master Hsu, letting him know Mei-hua had returned and requested an audience as soon as possible. Before long, Mei-hua was sitting across from Master Hsu in his study. Guei-lung hadn't returned, so Master Hsu hadn't learned anything of the day's misadventures, including Guei-lung's injury and Da-shan's arrest. Mei-hua filled him in on every detail as best she could.

Once assured that Guei-lung's arm was not seriously hurt, he seemed particularly interested in the men who ate at the noodle stall and questioned her closely on what they looked like and what they were doing there. Finally, Mei-hua had told him every detail she remembered. They sat in silence for a long time as

Master Hsu considered her story.

"You and Guei-lung have had a remarkable day, Mei-hua," he commented dryly. "But let's go back to the robbers on the way to the temple."

He called for an attendant to bring in the day's mail. After it was placed in front of him on the desk, he leafed through a pile of papers on his desk. In a few moments, he pulled one out and read it. "Here is the official police report of the robbery. The officer in charge thinks they may have been common thugs who could not pass up an opportunity to rob a small group carrying alms to the temple, but he is continuing to investigate. His men are following up on the thugs, but have not yet discovered anything of note."

He looked up at Mei-hua. "Do you have anything else to add? Anything you haven't told me?"

She shook her head, "No, except that even though the leader's voice was muted by the cloth over his face, he did use Mandarin." Then with conviction, she added, "I might recognize it again."

Master Hsu gazed at her thoughtfully. "Good. If you can remember the voice, then when the police find the guilty men, you should be able to identify at least one of them. Perhaps Guei-lung can add something. We need more information before going ahead on this."

He fell silent once more, thinking. Mei-hua sat still. So much had happened today. It seemed as if it would be impossible for her to forget so many terrible events; she felt as if every detail had been burned forever into her memory. But now, in such a short time, her memory was more jumbled than she had expected. The silence gave Magistrate Hsu time to reflect, and it gave her more time to review the crazy happenings, too.

"Have you heard of secret societies?" Master Hsu asked, breaking the silence.

Mei-hua's stomach tightened. Secret societies. Her mind flew to the attack on the road as she and Guei-lung traveled to the temple.

"Yes, a bit," she said, forming her words carefully. "Before our Emperor established the great Ming Dynasty only a few years ago, large criminal organizations developed out of gangs of men. They robbed, kidnapped, and killed for hire and profit."

Master Hsu nodded his head. "Uh-hum. You're right when you say they existed before the present dynasty. Many started out as religious or political organizations. Men tried to create for themselves a bit of stability at the end of the last dynasty when there was so much chaos and confusion. They banded together for self-protection. For some, the alternative to belonging to a secret society and stealing was starvation. When the new Chinese dynasty was established, most disbanded or were destroyed. But, unfortunately, a few remain even today.

"It is my belief a large, far-reaching secret society still exists. I'm not sure, but it looks like Hangzhou might be the center for their activities. From what we can tell, the organization is spread throughout the central and southern region of the country. Your father ..."

Mei-hua flinched at his mentioning her father. Was he involved in this somehow? She remained silent, listening. She didn't have to wait long for the answer.

"... and I have been working together in an

attempt to discover the organization's structure and its leaders. It appears this secret society is widely spread geographically, and its members include the lowest and the highest placed people in our society."

Mei-hua listened carefully, but she couldn't imagine what all this had to do with her.

"Naturally, we've learned more about the people in the bottom levels of the society than we have about the leaders. In fact, we know very little about the leaders or who they are. From your descriptions of the men hanging around the noodle stand, it sounds like they may very well be a part of the society."

At this quiet declaration, Mei-hua's eyes opened wide and her head jerked to attention. "Secret society members here in Hangzhou, almost under the eaves of your own compound?"

He nodded, folding his hands in front of him on the desk. "It seems unbelievable. But the leader of this society is brilliant and fearless. Nothing seems to deter him."

"But what do they want? Are Mr. and Mrs. Mu in danger? Why would criminals be interested in them? Do you think Da-shan's one of them?" The questions tumbled from Mei-hua's lips.

Magistrate Hsu held up his hands, "Wait, wait. Patience."

When Mei-hua stopped her barrage of questions, he went on. "We are not sure what the secret society's goals are. Although we have our suspicions, we've nothing solid." He paused, silent for a moment, then continued, "As to the Mus, I'm afraid those men around their shop are gang members. Doctor Lum stopped in here after visiting the carpenter earlier today and he's convinced his illness isn't from natural causes. Though," he smiled at Mei-hua's startled look, "not from supernatural causes either. Before I say more on that, however, we must wait for the doctor to return with his analysis."

At these comments, Mei-hua remembered the small bottles she had with the remnants of Mr. Mu's medications. She took them out and handed them to Master Hsu while relating the story of how she came to have them.

"Good. You did the right thing, Mei-hua. I'm sure Doctor Lum will check on his patient as soon as he is able.

"That brings us to Da-shan. You say you believe him and his story of entering the religious life. You may be right. Certainly, such a large, tough man being overcome by a mere girl could be taken as a sign of celestial displeasure by almost anyone." Here Master Hsu exchanged a grin with Mei-hua. "And, quite frankly, I also agree with you when you say such a simple man would hardly devise a plan using the cover of a monk's life to rob people. His past history in crime is much more straight-forward: see something and take it. Quite direct and to the point."

"Why do you think Mr. Mien's customer lied about Da-shan stealing the money? Do you think he took it himself and this is just a cover-up?" Mei-hua asked.

"Could be. From your description, the eye witness sounds like one of the secret society members we've identified. One of their minions, a local thug. He could have taken the opportunity to rob and pass the blame on to Da-shan, who just happened to be there. A convenient patsy."

"Can you release Da-shan, Master Hsu? I would hate to have him in prison too long. He may suffer needlessly."

The magistrate shook his head, "Yes, sometimes our criminal system may seem cruel. I don't like guards torturing prisoners without good reason. But," he sighed, "sometimes it's the only way to get a criminal to confess. Many of these thieves and killers are tough and would never confess without such dire techniques. Unfortunately, we do have a few guards who use torture routinely with our prisoners." Master Hsu paused, took up a brush and quickly wrote out two orders. He folded them and called a waiting officer to his table. After murmuring a few words to him, the man strode from the room.

"I have just sent a message freeing Da-shan from prison. He's to return to Mr. Mu's and continue with his religious duties there. Also, I've ordered the arrest of the man who brought the false charges against him. We'll see what he says after a little time under the care of the prison guards!"

# CHAPTER 9

MEI-HUA SIGHED WITH RELIEF. True, Da-shan had lived a thieving life, but she truly believed he'd reformed. And if he were in the prison much longer, there was no doubt he would be tortured. She shuddered at the idea of his hands, arms, legs, or other bones being broken by guards trying to extract a confession. Under such circumstances, he might confess to put an end to his misery. Many innocent people did. What choice did they have? Only the magistrate had the power to release him in time to avoid such dire treatment.

One more question nagged Mei-hua until finally she had to ask.

"Sir, I don't mean to second-guess your decisions, but I wonder if I could ask you a question?"

Magistrate Hsu's eyebrows rose in a quizzical look. "And what would that be, Zhang Mei-hua?"

"The young soldier you sent along as a guard for me," she paused. "I do not mean to be impolite, but ..."

Interrupting her painful speech, Magistrate Hsu gave a hearty laugh. "You want to know something about your soldier, is that it?"

Mei-hua nodded, thankful she did not have to go

on. It was a sign of disrespect for young people to question the decisions or orders of their elders, and this went double for an official's order.

"Perhaps you think him an unlikely choice of a soldier."

Surprised he had guessed, Mei-hua still tried to protest because she didn't want him to think the young soldier had done something wrong. However, he leaned back in his chair, and continued before she could say anything.

"Actually, he's proven himself to be one of the best in military training. Capable and brilliant in strategy."

Mei-hua felt the warmth of embarrassment rise in her cheeks.

"Nevertheless, your assessment," here he grinned slightly, "is correct. For all his capabilities, his demeanor is, shall we say, too casual?

"Let me tell you something about him. He is the adopted son of Lord Chiu, who, among many other jobs, is head of the military administration in this region."

Mei-hua started. She'd heard a lot about Lord Chiu. Madam Wu had mentioned him, saying he protected their area. He was over the regional military and he'd cleaned up much of the local crime. More importantly, as a powerful eunuch, he had tremendous influence over the emperor.

She also remembered her father mentioning Lord Chiu. Although the details of what he'd said were now blurry. She recalled something about the eunuch's ruthless pursuit of power—and what a dangerous enemy he could be.

"Of course, eunuchs can't have children. But the desire for a son is natural in all men."

Mei-hua cringed at the implication that girls were not included, but remained silent.

Master Hsu went on, not noticing her slight discomfort, "Luckily for him, he had two brothers who each had several sons. It was easy for him to adopt his youngest brother's youngest son as his own. When the boy reached school age, he entered military training where, as I said, he excelled."

Mei-hua' eyes widened in surprise at this news. Master Hsu grinned again.

"You're amazed?"

"Well ..."

"You're right, as usual. For, while he excelled at military skills, he hasn't exhibited the proper military mentality. That is to say, he doesn't have the heart for battle. Thus, his father assigned him to my office to learn about the details of governing and law. Or so Lord Chiu tells me.

"I made him your guard because of his superior ability. In spite of his attitude, he'll do his best to protect you from harm. Since you are in my care as a member of my family, it's the least I can do for your father, my friend.

With this, Mei-hua understood Soldier Guo would be with her wherever she went. She was stuck with her unlikely soldier.

After thanking Master Hsu, Mei-hua told him she wanted to return to the Mu home. She planned to stay with Mrs. Mu through the night in case anything happened.

"No. You'll not go back there tonight; you're to stay here where it's safe."

"She needs me," Mei-hua blurted out.

"Sorry, it's not possible. However, you may return in the morning." At her petulant frown, he said, "Where would you—a single, young woman—sleep? They've no room, no bed, for you. I understand your desire to assist Mrs. Mu. However, if you're there, it'll only increase her anxiety. She'll feel the need to take care of you. In the midst of the pressure to take care of the Buddhist monks praying at the house and worrying about her sick husband, your added presence would be too much for her."

Mei-hua gave in. Since she must remain at the Hsu household tonight, she hurried over to the women's quarters. She briefly updated Madam Wu and Ping-an on the day's events and then went to her own room and slipped into bed. She didn't stay for supper; she was too tired to eat.

Guei-lung hadn't returned yet. As she fell into a deep sleep, she reminded herself to check on him in the morning before leaving for the Mus'.

*　*　*

As soon as Mei-hua arose, a maid helped her dress and tie her hair up in a fashionable knot. She wore no ornaments in her hair or on her dress. She didn't want to attract attention to herself, and, besides, it seemed inappropriate to wear jewelry and other ornaments when she was going to a dying man's home. Before she finished dressing, Orchid, Ping-an's maid, came in and told her Ping-an was awake and had ordered breakfast for the two of them.

Mei-hua smiled. "Ping-an's up early today."

"Um-hum, usually she likes to sleep in as late as possible, but she wanted to see you before you leave. Last night she dreamed you were in danger and she's afraid something will happen to you when you leave home."

"Well, I don't want her to worry about me. I'm not going far."

"The temple wasn't far either, yet you and Guei-lung managed to find a band of thieves," Orchid reminded her.

"Point well taken. I'll go right away. By the way, when did Guei-lung get home?"

"He came back quite late. I was already asleep. However, I heard he took Doctor Lum over to Mr. Mu's house before returning."

"Since he came back so late, I guess he's not awake yet."

"He's up and having breakfast with his mother. Master Hsu already left for work." She shook her head. "It seems that everyone is up early today. It's as if you're all expecting something to happen."

Mei-hua laughed, "You are as superstitious as Ping-an! It's no wonder she believes in all that stuff. You shouldn't encourage her. You know how sensitive she is."

"I can't help what's true," Orchid returned defensively.

Mei-hua made a wry face but said no more. Arguing was useless.

After the maid fussed over her a bit more, Mei-hua hurried to Ping-an's room. Ping-an sat on the kang while one of her maids combed her long, luxurious hair. She wore a pale green morning jacket over her matching night clothes. Her little lotus feet encased in flowered slippers peeked demurely out from under her flowing night wear. Looking at Ping-an, Mei-hua thought she could have stepped out of a classic Chinese painting of the feminine ideal.

"Mei-hua!" Ping-an cried out. Her face lit up in a smile. "I must tell you of the dream I had last night!" With this greeting, Ping-an pointed to a cushion next to her, encouraging Mei-hua to sit. Even before Mei-hua accepted the seat, the delicate girl began recounting her dream.

"You were taken to the world of the dead," Ping-an said with quiet excitement. Speaking out loud of dying and the dead was unlucky, and Ping-an whispered so any spirits in the room wouldn't hear her and bring bad luck to Mei-hua.

"Guei-lung was there, too. He kept saying there was a mistake; it wasn't your time to die." Her eyes opened wide and round as she muttered this to Mei-hua. "The spirits of the dead wouldn't listen. Mr. and Mrs. Mu stood near you, silent and resigned. Another man, wearing an apron, gave the spirits orders to take you away, and they dragged you down into the netherworld.

"Mei-hua you must be careful. I am certain my dream's a warning to you." Ping-an took her friend's hand and squeezed it. "Why don't you stay here today? Mr. and Mrs. Mu don't need you. They have the monks and Doctor Lum. What can you do? Stay here. It's safer at home."

Mei-hua was touched by Ping-an's fear for her

safety, but she had to go. What kind of person would she be if she didn't assist Mrs. Mu, who'd done so much for her? She owed the couple a great debt.

"Ping-an, I appreciate your concern, but I'm in no danger. Mr. Mu's illness is not contagious; I won't get sick. Yes, strange things have happened lately. Like the robbers we ran into on the way to the temple. That's part of what's bothering you, isn't it?" she said looking deeply into Ping-an's worried eyes.

She nodded at Mei-hua, a shadow crossing her face.

"Don't worry. I promise I'll be fine. I won't be outside the city walls; I'm just going around the block to the carpenter's shop. It's not far and really is perfectly safe."

"But Mei-hua ..."

"You know, I think your dream was about the past, not about the future," she said, trying to ease the girl's anxiety. Not only did she not want to worry Ping-an, but she also didn't want Ping-an to go to her mother with her worries. If Madam Wu became more concerned about her safety, it'd be impossible for Mei-hua to leave the house. The elderly couple was like family to her. They needed her now and she couldn't allow Ping-an's fears to get in the way.

After some time, Mei-hua managed to alleviate Ping-an's anxiety. "Let's go see your mother. Orchid said Guei-lung is with her, so we can find out what happened with Doctor Lum last night."

Ping-an quickly agreed and immediately began to dress while Mei-hua finished her breakfast. Soon the two friends left. Walking over to Madam Wu's rooms,

Ping-an steadied herself on her tiny feet by holding onto Mei-hua's arm.

Just as Orchid had said, Guei-lung sat eating breakfast with his mother. As soon as Mei-hua and his sister came in, he started telling them about Doctor Lum. When he had gone to his home yesterday, Doctor Lum was out on a call. After waiting for some time, the doctor returned and immediately went with Guei-lung to Mr. Mu's. Mrs. Mu told them the local practitioner happened to be in the house when her husband had a turn for the worse and was able to prescribe some medicine. Mei-hua gave it to her husband and he's been sleeping ever since. At first the news appeared to dismay the doctor, but after examining the sick man, he was reassured because his health appeared stable. He asked about the medicines, but Mrs. Mu could tell him nothing. He told the carpenter's wife to let her husband rest and, once again, admonished her to only give him the medicines he himself prescribed.

Mei-hua listened intently to his story. When he'd finished, she told Guei-lung she'd only pretended to administer the tonic to Mr. Mu. Instead, she'd poured most of it out. The remaining dregs she'd placed in a couple of small bottles for Doctor Lum to examine.

Guei-lung laughed, "I should have known you'd figure out something to get around giving him the medicine."

"What did you do with the bottles?" Madam Wu asked.

"I've turned them over to the magistrate."

Madam Wu nodded. "Good, he'll take care of it."

Both Guei-lung and Mei-hua were anxious to

leave. Although she had no fear for her own safety, Mei-hua was concerned about the old carpenter. She sensed something dangerous surrounded him and threatened his life. She didn't know who, what, why, or how the danger existed, but she knew she needed to find out before he was killed.

Promising to be careful, the two left the Hsu household in their palanquins. Soldier Guo once again loped ahead of them, leading the way. Mei-hua thought ruefully of how easy it was to travel as one of the regular folk—to just walk out the door and down the street. The upper classes traveled by palanquin, which took a lot longer for the same distance and involved more people. Four strong men were needed to carry each palanquin and at least one servant strode in front, keeping people on the streets out of their way. Clearly, it wasn't possible to be secretive in their movements. While they were behind curtains and couldn't be seen, who they were and where they were going was common knowledge before they even left the household gates.

*Nothing moves information faster than gossip,* Mei-hua observed to herself.

Just as the palanquins entered the street, they stopped. Hearing the *clack-clack-clack* of castanets, Mei-hua peeked out of the curtained window. The gates of the house hadn't been closed yet. A drunken beggar wearing only one boot danced and sang in front of her carriage. A crowd of people watched, filling the street. In his drunken dance, he clapped a pair of castanets as long as her arm. He swung a basket of flowers at his side. Catching her eye behind the curtain, the beggar turned and sang to her:

Which will live longer
a majestic tree admired by all,
or the grass beneath our footfall?
Answering his own riddle, he laughed in Mei-
hua's direction and gleefully sang out:
When the wind blows
the tree must break,
the grass must bend.
for the one there will be a wake,
the other's life will never end.

# CHAPTER 10

MEI-HUA SHIVERED, although whether because of the man's bizarre behavior or because she was feeling vulnerable, she didn't know. He resembled one of the Immortals she saw in the temple's mural, the one carrying a long castanet and a basket of flowers. Even in the painting, he'd looked carefree and full of fun. She trembled again. He may look like the Immortal in the mural, but this fellow's words were neither joyful nor amusing. Yet, they struck a chord with her.

Mei-hua glanced down, overcome with emotion. When she looked up again, she found he had disappeared. The dust and noise of the street hung heavily about her palanquin. Even so, the song and riddle repeated themselves over and over in her mind. Automatically, her hand dropped over the jade amulet she always wore beneath her jacket. It lay cool against her skin. Did he know about the amulet and its inscription, "When the wind blows the grass must bend," or were his mutterings a mere coincidence? Her eyes searched the street, but he was gone. She'd never know.

As she considered this strange incident, her palanquin once again began rhythmically rocking back and forth. Her body swayed with the movement of the men carrying her and Mei-hua finally put aside the beggar and his poem. She gave herself up to working out the problem of Mr. and Mrs. Mu.

After talking with Master Hsu, she began to believe something more sinister lay behind Mr. Mu's illness. Why would anyone plot to kill the carpenter? He owned nothing beyond his small shop. He and his wife worked hard and shared a simple life. A life they would lose if he couldn't work.

With these thoughts bouncing through her head, they reached the shop. No female attendants had come with her because she had assured Madam Wu they would only be in the way within the smaller spaces of the Mu's home. Therefore, when the door opened for her to step outside, Soldier Guo stood nearby holding his hand out to assist her. Mei-hua was taken aback by this presumptive behavior. Young men, even servants, didn't normally come into direct contact with the women of the house where they worked.

Just as she was about to draw back, however, she caught the laughing—or was it mocking?—twinkle in his dark eyes. She instantly met the unspoken challenge and, with a glance of defiance, took his outstretched hand. She would show him that his unconventional behavior did not intimidate her. She laid her hand in his open palm. As his fingers closed around it, she became keenly aware of the strength and warmth emanating from his hand and into hers. The surge of energy spread up her arm and through her body. She dropped her eyes. The sudden flush of warmth made the innocent touch seem too intimate. Mei-hua had to look away.

Guei-lung, who had alighted simultaneously from his palanquin, strode over to her. His presence broke the spell. She stepped down as quickly as possible and released Guo's hand. Guei-lung flashed a look of annoyance at the young soldier, and then, stepping between them, waited for Mei-hua to enter the shop first.

As she began to move forward, another tattered beggar carrying a gourd limped up to them on an iron crutch. Stopping within inches of Mei-hua, he squinted up at her, for his crooked back made his head lower than hers. In a bottomless, solemn voice he announced, "Truth is to jade as falseness is to dust. Without truth there is death."

Without waiting for a reply, or even a reaction, the vagrant slowly turned and limped away.

Guei-lung and Mei-hua stared at each other, startled.

Guei-lung spoke first, "Hey, that man ... we've seen him before."

"You're right! He's the same man we met yesterday on the way to Mr. Mu's. He spoke of truth and dying then, too." She shook her head as she watched the bent form melt into the crowd. She thought of the Abbot and what he'd said to her. Could this really be Iron Crutch Lu? Was the other apparition—for what else could he have been?—another of the Eight Immortals? It seemed impossible.

"A morbid kind of fellow, if you ask me," Guei-lung said.

"But, what did he mean? What about truth and dying?" She hesitated to tell Guei-lung what she was beginning to really think: that this beggar could be an Immortal. Now, away from the spiritual atmosphere surrounding the Abbot and the temple, it even sounded farfetched to her. Almost.

"Our city is filling up with these crazies. First, the drunken dancer parading around in front of your palanquin and now this crippled beggar. Really, it's time to clean up the streets. Get rid of these people. I'm going to speak to Father when we get back. He can do something about this rabble."

"Um-hum. Talking to Master Hsu is a good idea," Mei-hua responded. He needed to hear about these incidents. Their appearance seemed too coincidental and their behavior too bizarre for them to be common, everyday, beggars. She hadn't mentioned the first incident to him because it seemed unimportant at the time, just an unfortunate, crazy vagrant. And, of course, if she had mentioned that the man might be an Immortal, he would never take her seriously.

Now, however, she was beginning to wonder: Were these encounters connected? Were these two really street people? Or was the Abbot's suggestion right and they were Immortals trying to warn her? But warn her of what?

"Guei-lung, did these men seem at all familiar to you? Do you think you might have ever met them, or seen, say, a picture or something of them?"

Guei-lung looked aghast. "Never! Except for that unfortunate meeting the other day, when would my path ever cross with the likes of them?"

Mei-hua sighed, nodded, and—carefully avoiding Soldier Guo—walked into the Mu shop without another comment. She resolved to discuss this with Master Hsu as soon as they returned home. In the meantime, she was going to be alert. Did these strangers know something about her or this situation and were they warning her? She shook her head. How beggars would know anything about her was a mystery in itself. Still, she would be on her guard and not take anyone at their word. She would look for what is true and what is not.

Upon entering the shop, perfumed air pulsated around them. The sweet, powerful scent came from the left side of the front room where the saffron-robed Buddhist monks once again included Da-shan. They sat cross-legged burning incense sticks and chanting in low, rhythmic voices. No sooner had they entered than Mrs. Mu rushed over, greeting them.

"Aren't they doing a fine job?" she asked thrusting her head in a quick motion in the monks' direction. "They've been praying continuously since they arrived. Even Da-shan." She glanced over at the enormous monk sitting head up, eyes straight ahead, praying in a monotonous voice. "He returned yesterday evening, just after the police arrested one of Mr. Mien's customers. They said he falsely accused Da-shan of theft. Imagine that!" She then proceeded to tell Mei-hua and Guei-lung of last night's events. Mei-hua already knew what happened, but, out of respect, she listened as the older woman told her story.

Finally, finishing the numerous details of what happened, Mrs. Mu mentioned Mr. Mien's suggestion of bringing in a Taoist priest. Keep the monks, of course; it would double her husband's chances of regaining his health. Plus, through divination, the priest would discover the cause of Mr. Mu's illness. By doing this, there would be no stone unturned in finding a solution for Mr. Mu: an excellent medical doctor was treating him; the Buddhist monks were praying for his health; and now a Taoist priest could find the root cause of this inexplicable sickness. "Naturally," she said with a note of hope, "I told Mr. Mien to bring in a Taoist priest."

Mei-hua stared at Mrs. Mu in surprise.

"A Taoist priest? When will you bring him here?" Mei-hua asked. She hoped her calm tone hid her shock at this new development. While it was true that her father never said anything bad about other people's religious beliefs, it was clear he didn't believe in most of the Taoist ghosts and spirits. At the same time, he also praised the ideas in Taoism, saying they could be used to guide one's life. He clearly separated Taoist philosophy from its many supernatural beings.

"Oh, he's here already, my child," Mrs. Mu said smiling. "He's in with Mr. Mu right now."

Mei-hua hurried into the back room with Guei-lung and Mrs. Mu trailing behind. Soldier Guo was the last to follow. Upon entering the sick man's room, Mei-hua saw a figure leaning over the carpenter's still form. As they watched, he straightened up and raised his arms, hands open. Possessed and chanting loudly in the language of spirits, he swept his hands several times over the sick man. Mei-hua had seen such treatments before and always found them disconcerting. Yet there was something about this priest specifically that nagged at her. His voice seemed familiar.

For a long time he chanted and called out,

pushing and kneading the air about the patient. Then he stopped, turned around to face them, and shook his head as if in a daze. He was coming out of the trance.

No. She didn't recognize him. His voice was familiar, but not his face.

Silently, the priest's assistant helped him sit, where he remained slumped on a stool in silence for several minutes. After such a spirit possession, he was exhausted. The trance appeared to have taken every ounce of his strength. Neither the priest nor his assistant took any notice of the four silent figures standing just within the doorway. The musical chanting of the Buddhist monks in the next room provided a backdrop of soothing tones.

Eventually, the priest started to straighten his back, but he remained on the stool. "Bring me some wine," he ordered in a strong voice.

Mei-hua's head snapped up. His order immediately brought an image of the robbers outside the Misty Temple. That voice! It belonged to their leader!

# CHAPTER 11

SHE HADN'T SEEN HIS FACE, but she'd heard his voice as he barked orders to his men in a clear Mandarin dialect. Could this really be him? Why was he here? She shot a glance at Guei-lung and then Soldier Guo. Guei-lung was observing the Taoist priest with keen interest, but he didn't seem to recognize him. Soldier Guo stood with his feet apart, resting his weight on his spear, looking more bored than anything. As she observed the young man, he turned his head and caught her gaze. The twinkle reappeared in his eyes and a slight smile touched his lips. His look conveyed a sense of playfulness, not the recognition of an enemy in their midst.

Mei-hua gazed at the priest once more. Her father used to say that trauma could color what and how people remembered things, especially when they are the victims of a crime, and the attempted robbery had been chaotic and shocking. How could she trust her own memories of such a moment, particularly when no one else seemed to share her suspicions? Could she really be so mistaken?

She continued observing him as he went through his ritual. *Wait*, she admonished herself. *Wait.*

She watched the man's quiet face as he drank wine from a bowl his assistant placed in his hands. Watched as he took a wet towel from the assistant and told him to gather the sacred materials into a bundle. She shook her head. Whether she shared his beliefs or not, this priest appeared to be a devout man who took his duties seriously. The idea that such a person would also be a highway robber, or try to harm a young man he'd never met, was ridiculous. She must be wrong. Lots of people spoke Mandarin, the language of the educated and the government. It could not have been his voice she heard calling to the other bandits.

*It's just a coincidence—or a trick of my imagination—that he sounds similar.* Mei-hua told herself. *Wasn't this what the beggars were warning me about: of mistaking the false for the truth? Maybe this is what they meant.*

While Mei-hua engaged in this internal discussion, the Taoist wiped his face once, twice, three times with the towel using large circular motions. He dropped the towel and stepped up to Mrs. Mu, ignoring the others in the room.

"Madam," he said in a deep, hollow voice which made Mei-hua shiver, "your husband's condition is quite serious. The spirits of hell are calling for his soul. He's using all of his strength to resist, but he can't last much longer without help."

Mrs. Mu's small form stiffened. She had readied herself, preparing for bad news and ready to fight for her husband's soul. The aura of defeat and hopelessness that surrounded her earlier was gone. Her face had hardened, showing strength and resolve. Mei-hua thought perhaps her friend felt more able to deal with spirits and their whims than with sickness and disease.

"Without help," Mrs. Mu repeated. "What kind of help does he need? We can do whatever is necessary." Mei-hua, standing at her side, reached out a hand to support the frail older woman's arm.

"Before you can do anything, you must understand what has happened. As you know," he began explaining, "the officials in the netherworld keep a book with all the names of the living and, next to each name, the dates when they will die."

Mrs. Mu nodded but remained silent.

"Originally, your husband's date for entering the netherworld was recorded fifteen years from today. He would have lived for fifteen more years. However, with his work as a carpenter, he has made many, many caskets. Each casket took time off his life span. So now, the spirit in charge of the book insists he leave this earth and enter the netherworld. The spirit claims that through his work he has canceled fifteen years of his life."

Although Mrs. Mu continued to stand straight, Mei-hua could feel her body tremble slightly at these words. Clearly, it took all of her resolve to hold fast. The troubled woman said nothing and simply nodded at this distressful news.

Raising his right hand above his head, palm toward Mrs. Mu, he continued. "This is not an unusual case, but it is quite difficult, as you can imagine. The spirits of the dead are always trying to shorten the lives of those of us up here. Fortunately, I discovered the problem in time. I can still save your husband. But," he added just as Mrs. Mu was about to speak, "the process is dangerous and I must have your complete trust and confidence. Is that clear?" With these final words he squinted his eyes and peered at her, pausing for an answer.

"Yes, I will do whatever you say, whatever the cost. Mr. Mu will be saved!" she stammered holding back the tears.

"Good. That is good."

The Taoist crossed over to the seat near Mr. Mu's bed, picked up the three-legged stool and moved it nearer to the carpenter's wife, who was still standing within the doorway.

Sitting down, he continued. "Retrieving his soul from hell and returning him to good health requires another soul to take his place. The damage has already been done. He made the caskets, there is no denying that. So, another soul must go in his stead. It can't be just any soul either. The soul must come from someone who owes Mr. Mu a tremendous debt, someone whose life has been changed for the better by this man."

"Someone else must go?" she repeated and shivered, disbelieving. "Someone else will ... die?"

"No, no. Not necessarily. The other person must give up fifteen years of his or her life span to replace those your husband lost. Of course, if that person had fifteen years or less to live, yes, he or she would die. But, if he or she had more years to live, his or her life would be shortened by fifteen years. That person would still be allowed to remain on earth however many years there are left after deducting the fifteen they have traded."

Listening to this, Mei-hua wondered if every

time he said "or her" he stressed the "her." The carpenter's wife appeared relieved at the Taoist priest's final remarks. She smiled and said, "Why, this is no problem at all! He is my husband and my life is his. I owe him everything. I shall enter to the netherworld instead of him. Nothing could be easier."

"No, no, madam. The spirits of the dead would never accept a mere wife in replacement of such a man."

Mrs. Mu began to argue her case, but was interrupted by Mr. Mien who had slipped in without anyone noticing him.

"There is one obvious person, whose soul could give up fifteen years for Mr. Mu and who owes him such a debt," he said.

"Who would that be, Mr. Mien?" the distraught wife asked in surprise.

"Why, Mei-hua, of course. Hasn't she gained much through the intervention of Mr. Mu? Although she is a mere girl, and would not normally count for much, the good priest here did indicate the replacement soul could be a girl or a woman. Isn't that so, Sir?"

"Yes, while a wife could never be considered, I could convince the spirits of the dead to take another female's soul. As long as she owed Mr. Mu a significant debt of gratitude." The Taoist's entire upper body moved up and down, sagely agreeing with the suggestion.

"Well, Mei-hua would never be a guest living in the honorable house of Magistrate Hsu, and running around without constraints, if it weren't for Mr. Mu," the noodle stall owner said. He cast a penetrating stare, demanding agreement, at Mei-hua.

"Wait a minute," Guei-lung interrupted, "I'm

sure lots of people owe him a debt. Mei-hua's not the only one. Why should she do this?"

Mrs. Mu patted Mei-hua's hand resting on her arm. "No one is going to allow Mei-hua to give up her soul's time for Mr. Mu, Guei-lung. Don't you worry. I know my husband would never stand for such a thing. He would give his life for her. He would never expect, or want, her to give her life for him. She is like a daughter to us."

"Yes, and a daughter's duty is to do whatever is needed for her parents," Mr. Mien said. "It is her filial duty."

"What are you trying to do, Mr. Mien?" Guei-lung lashed out angrily.

During this discussion, Mei-hua remained quiet, listening, thinking. "It's all right, Guei-lung," she finally said. "Is that true, sir? Can you make the spirits of the dead accept my soul in place of Mr. Mu's?"

"Yes. Naturally, such a task will be difficult. The spirits, as with us, don't count a female soul to be as worthy as a male soul." Mei-hua winced, but held her tongue. "Still, if she owes Mr. Mu her changed fortunes, then I have the power and ability to convince the spirits to make the replacement."

"What will happen to her?" Mrs. Mu asked, distressed at this awful choice. "Will she be in pain?"

The Taoist priest paused, he never looked at Mei-hua, even now. "She will not experience pain. Most likely one of two things will happen, Madam. One, the spirits of the dead will accept the trade, but as a mere female they may require she offer more than fifteen years worth of life to replace a man's time. How much more time, I cannot say. I must negotiate the time she needs to give up with the spirits. Two, we don't know how much time Mei-hua has herself. If she has less than the time needed to trade for Mr. Mu's life, she will have to remain in the netherworld. If such is the case, when the spirits take her, she will only feel a prick on her skin as her spirit leaves her body."

Both Guei-lung and Mrs. Mu started at this last statement. Soldier Guo narrowed his eyes and watched Mei-hua with concern.

Mei-hua broke the stunned silence. "I will do whatever is necessary, sir. I am prepared to give my soul's time for Mr. Mu's."

# CHAPTER 12

IT WAS EASY for Mei-hua to accept this challenge. Her father took a rational view of the world and encouraged his daughter to do the same. While firm in his beliefs, he also reminded her that it was important to respect the right of others to have different points of view.

She was confident the spirits wouldn't kill her or take years off her life. Although most people knew of the spirit ledger, with the date of each person's death, she personally wasn't completely convinced of its existence. Her father encouraged her to learn and follow Confucius as a guide for how to be a full and good person. She didn't know what happened when a person died since Confucius himself didn't speak about this question, leaving it up to each person to decide. Still, she didn't believe this man could change the time of her natural death. And, as for any earthly dangers, Soldier Guo and Guei-lung were right here to protect her. She was sure she had nothing to lose in going through with the ceremony. Therefore, if in offering her soul to replace her friend's lost time would bring Mrs. Mu some peace—until Doctor Lum could cure him—she felt it was a small price to pay.

As a result, she was unprepared for what

happened next.

Once she told the medium she was willing to help Mr. Mu, he immediately sent for two more assistants and began preparations for the ceremony. For the next couple of hours, as Mei-hua, Guei-lung, and Mrs. Mu sat near Mr. Mu, talking in low voices, the medium and his assistants arranged offerings on a table with which to bribe the spirits. They used a fistful of fragrant herbs to sweep the floor, which, after generations of use, was firmly compacted by daily cleaning and sweeping. Its smooth, hard-packed surface swallowed the sounds of their quickly moving feet.

While Mei-hua and the others watched, the men carefully formed a pile of twigs in the center of a circle formed by several pots. One assistant placed a bamboo carrying pole with a wok cooking pan attached to it against a wall. The wok clanged as it hit the wood and finally rested at a strange angle.

As streaks of the evening sun's light began moving across the kitchen floor, the medium, dressed in common workers' clothing, wrapped a lengthy white cloth around his waist. He murmured to his assistant, who instantly approached Mei-hua and asked her to come and sit on a low stool between the offering table and the circle of pots in the center of the room. Guei-lung once more tried to stop her, but she interrupted him with a quick shake of her head and a glance toward Mr. Mu. He stopped, apparently understanding her need to help her friends in whatever way possible. Nevertheless, as she stood to follow the assistant, Guei-lung reached out and momentarily held her hand. Mrs. Mu took her other hand.

"It'll be all right," Mei-hua told them both, smiling. "I'm not afraid and neither of you should be, either." With this, she strode over to the stool and sat down. The assistant directed her to turn her body so she faced the circle of pots.

Soldier Guo moved away from the wall and took up a position a few feet from her. He remained out of the medium's way but close enough to come to her aid, if needed.

The medium murmured in a voice too low for the others to understand. Once he finished, the assistant instructed everyone to remain where they were. The ceremony began. One of the assistants lit long, thin sticks of incense. Others began a regular, hypnotic rhythm by beating on a drum and two gongs. The rhythm produced an incongruous harmony with the chanting of the Buddhist monks in the next room. The Taoist drum and gongs intensified the beat until the two rhythms joined and became almost palpable.

Even as the first assistant spoke, the medium—wrapped in the rising swirls of incense—stood across from Mei-hua on the other side of the pots. He started chanting, swaying his body slightly, eyes closed. Although she'd never participated in such a ceremony before, she knew the medium was going into a trance; his body would become a bridge to the spiritual world. Spirits from the other world would communicate with them directly by possessing his mortal body.

While he prayed, the room dimmed as the last light of day slid away. Before the room became totally engulfed in darkness, however, another assistant lit the small mound of twigs in the center of the pot circle.

Bright flames danced up and down, casting an eerie light over the room and the people in it.

Mei-hua rested her eyes on Mr. Mu's still form. He looked even paler than before. She was glad she agreed to do this. Even if he died, Mrs. Mu would have the satisfaction of knowing Mei-hua, who she thought of as a daughter, did everything possible to save him. At this thought, tears welled up in her eyes and her vision blurred. She wondered whether Doctor Lum could actually help. In truth, although she tried to not allow the idea to surface in her mind, she feared her carpenter friend wouldn't make it through the night.

Once again, the light in the room grew gloomy and dimmed as the fire died down to glowing embers. An assistant picked up the bamboo pole and its wok and carried it over to the medium. Then he held the pole parallel to the ground, allowing the wok to dangle. Mesmerized by its swinging motion, Mei-hua shuddered. It seemed to mark the moments Mr. Mu had left before he passed into the netherworld.

Still chanting, the medium picked up one of the pots and poured several inches of a liquid into the wok. Taking one end of the bamboo pole, the medium and his assistant held the wok low over the embers. As the liquid warmed, the medium called out in a loud voice. Neither Mei-hua nor any of the others understood him. He spoke in the language of the spirits which no human, except mediums and some of their assistants, understood. Crying out once more, the medium swung his free hand over the wok and a flame shot into the air, momentarily lighting up the faces of all present.

Both Guei-lung and Mrs. Mu's eyes were wide

and staring. Mei-hua was also taken by surprise and stared spellbound at the wok's flame. Only Soldier Guo remained vigilant. His eyes kept roving around Mei-hua, alert for possible danger.

Almost as quickly as it appeared, the flame disappeared, leaving a column of smoke in its place. A nearby assistant handed the medium one of the carpenter's chisels. Still holding onto one end of the pole and chanting rhythmically, he took the chisel and passed it several times in a wide arc through the smoke. Mei-hua looked around and noticed a pile of Mr. Mu's tools and clothes at the feet of another assistant standing near the medium. The Taoist priest needed to purify each piece. The purification would allow Mr. Mu to continue working after his recovery without bad karma continuing to build up. If the bad karma did build up again, the carpenter would be faced with the same problem of dying before his natural time.

For each of the items in the pile, the medium prayed loudly, passed his hand over the liquid in the wok, and caused a flame of fire to burst out. When the fire disappeared, he passed a knife, awl, work apron, and other tools through the resulting column of purifying smoke. He rapidly cleansed each tool and piece of clothing in the mound before him.

During this part of the ceremony, the room filled with a murky, dark haze. Mei-hua's eyes stung; her breath came in gulps. Guei-lung and Mrs. Mu had disappeared, even though they were but a few yards away. Soldier Guo looked like a slightly darker space in the room, nothing more. Even the fire's glowing embers, just feet from where she sat, had faded into fitful points of red.

With the drum and gong keeping time and the chanting filling her ears, Mei-hua began to feel disoriented. Something stung the back of her neck. As she reached up to touch the spot where she felt the light prick, she lost control. No longer able to maintain her balance, she was aware of her body slumping over and slowly tumbling sideways onto the floor. There she lay, unnoticed, a rumpled mass in the darkened, smoky room.

# CHAPTER 13

LYING ON THE FLOOR, Mei-hua struggled to get up. None of her muscles responded, not even a twinge. All of the sounds around her remained perfectly clear: the steady beating of the Taoist's drum and gong, his chanting, and the more removed sounds of the Buddhist monks' prayers in the adjoining room. She heard *cchr-cchr, cchr-cchr* as someone moved around behind her, perhaps bringing more liquid for the wok. But she remained paralyzed. She was aware that she was on the floor, bent like a loose knot, but she felt nothing. Helpless, she had no control over her own body, nor was she able to see. Yet, strange as it seemed, whatever happened to her hadn't affected her ears. She heard everything perfectly.

Soon she heard the *whoosh* of the flame as it burst from the wok. Almost instantaneously Mrs. Mu called out, "Mei-hua!"

"Don't touch her! Move back, soldier! Get back!" commanded the medium. "Her soul has left her. If you disturb her now, it may not come back."

"But can't we at least lay her back on the cot?" Mrs. Mu asked in dismay.

"We must leave her. Her soul is in the hands of

the spirits. Are you willing to take a chance with her life by angering them?"

"No." Mrs. Mu was still cowed by the authority with which the medium spoke.

"Good. Know this is a good sign. Her soul is in the netherworld now. I will enter another trance and follow her down. Leave this to me; I will negotiate the release of both her soul and Mr. Mu's."

"Yes, yes. Go!" Mrs. Mu cried out with a sob.

For what seemed an interminable time, the sounds in the room didn't allow Mei-hua to figure out exactly what the medium was doing. She heard scuffling feet, pottery hitting against pottery, as well as the *scree-scree* of containers being shoved about. Periodically, the medium spoke in the unintelligible spirit language. Sometimes he seemed to be begging and other times to be demanding.

After a long time, Mei-hua guessed more than an hour, he murmured, "Yes, yes," in a low voice, as if agreeing with an unseen and unheard other person. Then all was quiet. There were no sounds from anyone. The silence filled the room and all of its corners.

Finally, the medium sighed and let out a long, releasing breadth. Exhausted, he said, "It's all right. The spirits of the dead didn't want to take her worthless years in exchange for Mr. Mu's. But I've convinced them."

"Will she be all right? Will she live?" Mrs. Mu asked in a soft, tearful voice.

"That part is still being considered."

"What the ..." Guei-lung said.

"Wait, Guei-lung, wait," Mrs. Mu tried to mollify

him. Mei-hua heard a confusion of people moving about. She guessed Mrs. Mu was trying to keep Guei-lung sitting quietly.

"Don't be alarmed young Master." the Taoist's silky voice broke over the wash of random noises. "Trust me. I will take care of this. We will hold another ceremony and offer new prayers and gifts for the spirits. If they accept our offerings, they will allow her to remain among us."

"What kind of offerings?" Guei-lung demanded, anger bleeding through every word.

"Be careful young Master. You do not want to offend the spirits and make them angry. You know they hear everything."

"I know no such thing!"

"Guei-lung! Please, try to remain calm. This is for Mei-hua. We *must* do whatever is necessary," Mrs. Mu pleaded.

"Well, let's at least get her up on a decent cot! Leaving her on the dirt floor like that is unseemly!"

"Of course," the medium responded. He ordered his assistants to pick her up and lay her on another cot placed against the far wall. Mrs. Mu slept here each night, so as not to disturb her husband as he lay sick in their bed.

"I'll do it," a low, mellow voice interrupted the commands. Mei-hua recognized Soldier Guo's voice. Then she heard the sounds of his breath close to her face as he picked her up and laid her on the cot.

She heard Mrs. Mu shuffle over to the cot and then the gentle *swup, swup, swup* of material against material. Mei-hua guessed she was spreading a small blanket over her.

"I am taking her home where she can get proper care!" Guei-lung announced.

"That is not a good idea. She must not be separated from Mr. Mu. Their souls are both at risk; the one influences the life chances of the other," the priest said.

"Nonsense! She must go home and be properly cared for by Doctor Lum."

"Young Master, Doctor Lum is an honorable and remarkable doctor, but his medicines will not help Mei-hua's trouble. She needs spiritual assistance, not medical assistance."

"Yes, Guei-lung. The good Taoist priest is right. Leave Mei-hua here where he can perform the life-saving rituals for her and my husband. They will both be back with us soon!"

"This is impossible! With all due respect Madam Mu, I cannot go back to my father and mother and tell them I left Mei-hua here, unconscious, perhaps at the point of death. She will go back with me!"

"Mrs. Mu, make him listen. He could kill her by moving her while her soul is still in the netherworld. When it comes back and doesn't find her body, she will die for sure."

"Guei-lung, listen to us. I love Mei-hua, too. She will be safe here with me. My place is plain, but she will be well cared for and the honorable priest can perform the rituals as they should be done. Her guard can remain here, if you'd like."

"This is absurd!"

"I know that you question whether her collapse

is a sickness of the body or comes from the power of the spirits, but look what's happened! Mei-hua was strong and healthy before the ceremony started, and now she's lifeless! Don't you believe your own eyes? Without this priest she'll certainly die!" Mrs. Mu again desperately pleaded with the young man.

"I must take her back to my parent's home!" With these words, the *thump-thump-thump* of boots grew louder, then stopped.

"Don't pick her up! Don't take her away," the carpenter's wife said, sobbing softly.

"I'll carry her for you, young Master Hsu," Soldier Guo said.

"Take her. We must leave," Guei-lung ordered. "I am sorry, Mrs. Mu. I know you mean well, but she will go with me."

"Her fate's now in your hands, young Master," the medium intoned solemnly.

"Humph," was Guei-lung's only response.
After this, Mei-hua was conscious of the sounds of shoes, a door creaking open, and orders given to the palanquin carriers. They were taking her back to Guei-lung's home.

# CHAPTER 14

MEI-HUA HAD HOPED that given a little time her symptoms would abate. However, she soon realized nothing had changed. Her hope began to fade and her frustration grew. As much as she wanted to indicate that she was conscious, it was impossible. Her body was in a catatonic state. She wasn't able to communicate by speaking, moving, or even blinking. Fortunately, for some reason she didn't understand, she was still able to hear clearly. And so it was through hearing, and hearing only, that she guessed at what was happening.

How long would she be a prisoner in her own body? The idea of being trapped, incapacitated, for the rest of her life was overwhelming. In defense, she forced her total concentration on the sounds of activities and conversations around her. Anything to avoid thinking about what it would be like to spend the rest of her life as a vegetable.

She heard Soldier Guo's breathing close to her. Was he still holding her as the palanquin carried them to the Hsu household? Why would he be there? Finally, she realized that because she had no female attendant, his job as her guard was to keep her from falling helplessly onto the floor.

Periodically, he muttered, "Mei-hua, Mei-hua," in a low, mournful, barely audible voice. She wondered at the depth of sadness that came through his voice. More than anything, she wanted to be able to indicate she was alive—that she was here locked inside her own stiff, non-responding body—but she couldn't.

Once the palanquin stopped, following Guei-lung's orders, Soldier Guo carried her inside. Immediately, a rush of anxious and concerned voices came from every corner. Soon she heard cries of dismay from Madam Wu and Ping-an.

"Put her here, on the kang, and return to your post," Madam Wu ordered.

*Thump-thump-thump* told Mei-hua the young soldier left the private women's quarters.

Madam Wu sent a servant to alert Master Hsu. *He won't be able to come*, Mei-hua thought, *he must be in court. He can't leave his duties.*

"Fetch Doctor Lum," Madam Wu said. "Tell him he's needed immediately. Mei-hua is in critical condition."

Within a short time—although it seemed forever—the servant returned and said, "Doctor Lum is at Mr. Mu's shop. He will come as soon as he finishes."

There was nothing to do but wait. In the meantime, Guei-lung updated his mother and sister on the events that led Mei-hua to such a state, including all the details of the Taoist priest's séance and Mei-hua's agreement to offer her years for the carpenter's return. As soon as he finished recounting the story, his mother sent him out into the hall to wait for Doctor Lum.

"She has taken ill, that's all," Madam Wu said to

Ping-an after her son left. "She's spent too much time with that very sick man. Why would Mrs. Mu instantly accept that these troubles are anything else? We shouldn't immediately accept the Taoist's reasoning. It's clear how Mei-hua got sick. Mrs. Mu should know better. She seems too practical to rush to such conclusions."

"But *ma-ma*, look at what has happened to Mei-hua! Her collapse was sudden. A natural sickness wouldn't be like that. The spirits of the dead took her years and left her like this. She's barely alive. Perhaps they will not let her soul return to her body and she'll die!" Ping-an wailed.

"Ping-an, you're much too excitable," her mother said in a firm voice. "Doctor Lum can take care of whatever is wrong with Mei-hua. More than likely, she is suffering from exposure to her friend or to all the awful smoke Guei-lung told us about."

Madam Wu didn't say any more on the topic. Instead, she gave her attention over to making sure the servants took proper care of the apparently unconscious Mei-hua.

Guei-lung hurried, breathless, into the room. "Mother, Doctor Lum has arrived!"

Doctor Lum's voice came from the doorway just as the young man finished speaking. "Good evening, Madam," Doctor Lum pronounced before entering the room. "Forgive me for my tardiness, but I was just now attending to Mr. Mu as your husband requested."

"Yes, I quite understand, Doctor. Thank you for coming. How is Mr. Mu's health?"

Approaching Mei-hua, Doctor Lum said, "I

believe that I arrived there none too soon. I insisted the Taoist priest cease his work. Although Mrs. Mu was quite distraught at my orders, she agreed. There will be no more séances tonight."

"Thank goodness," Madam Wu responded. "Look what has happened to poor Mei-hua because of his infernal ritual."

"*Ma-ma*!" Ping-an cried.

"I am sorry, Ping-an, but I can't help feeling she would not be laying here now if it were not for that smoke in such closed quarters. It may have weakened her system and allowed Mr. Mu's sickness to seep into her, too. What do you think, Doctor Lum?"

With his voice very close to her ear, Mei-hua heard Doctor Lum say, "Her pulse is extremely weak, and she is just barely breathing. She appears to be in a coma." He paused. "I seriously doubt her illness is due to smoke inhalation." His voice moved away from Mei-hua.

After a lengthy silence, the doctor continued, "Madam, it is my opinion that although Mr. Mu and Mei-hua have different symptoms, they are from the same cause."

"Why, how could that be?" Madam Wu asked.

"Are you saying the spirits are behind these problems, Doctor Lum? Are they the one cause for two different illnesses?" Guei-lung asked.

"No. The spirits did not drag Mr. Mu and Mei-hua to death's door," Doctor Lum said. "Someone is poisoning them!"

# CHAPTER 15

"POISONED!" gasped Madam Wu, Guei-lung, and Ping-an in unison.

"How can that be? Why would anyone poison them? Explain what you mean, Doctor," Madam Wu demanded.

Mei-hua's heart sank. Would she be locked in this useless body forever? Or would she die sooner than she ever thought? Which was worse?

"Since I am only a doctor and not a judge, I cannot answer why someone would try to kill them. I can only say that someone has. I suspected Mr. Mu was poisoned on my first visit to his bedside, but I needed to study the matter further before making any charges." He needlessly added, "This is a very serious allegation."

He paused before continuing. "After careful examination of Mr. Mu's symptoms and of various possible toxins, I returned tonight to examine him again. I needed to confirm my suspicions. Unfortunately, I did not act quickly enough to prevent another poisoning: Mei-hua's."

"Yes, but Doctor, how can they both be poisoned when their illnesses appear so different? Mr. Mu has been ill for quite some time, and Mei-hua, poor dear, collapsed suddenly tonight and lies senseless on this bed," Madam Mu said.

"To understand how these two appear to have different illnesses when they are the same, one needs to understand the nature of the substance given to them. First, the poison acts by freezing a person's body. This is because it attacks their nerves, leaving them as you see Mei-hua: seemingly dead, yet alive. Second, the poison will cause different symptoms if given to the victims in small amounts over a long period of time as opposed to one, large dosage.

"In other words, Mr. Mu has been poisoned in incremental, tiny doses over a long period of time, so his health appears to have failed gradually. In this way, it is quite difficult to detect poison as the reason for his illness. Yes, quite difficult. In such a case, no one would think of looking for a poison. On the other hand, if it were given in a massive dose at one time, the person would immediately stop breathing, her heart would stop beating, and she would die."

"But Mei-hua isn't dead; she's in a coma," Madam Mu said.

"Mei-hua was given a large amount of poison but, because she is young and strong, it wasn't enough to kill her. Instead, the poison has incapacitated her. Whether this amount is enough to eventually bring about her death, or whether it would simply leave her in this death-in-life state, I do not yet know."

"Oh, no!" Ping-an sobbed.

"Is there nothing to be done for Mei-hua and Mr. Mu?" Madam Wu asked.

"I have already started the healing process for

Mr. Mu. Because he was poisoned gradually, I am returning him to normal health slowly. Unfortunately, with Mei-hua the problem is different. She was given a large dose at one time. In order to counteract this dosage level, I need to give her a special remedy—also in a large quantity. The problem is, while strong, she may not be strong enough to withstand the antidote's effects. She may die from the cure."

"Sir!" Madam Wu demanded, "Is this the only way?"

"Yes, Madam. I'm sorry. Without the antidote she may die soon, or remain as she is for a lengthy period of time before dying. With the antidote, she may return to us whole and alive, as before, or she may die."

Everyone remained frozen in silence.

"What do you wish me to do?"

"You must give her the antidote immediately," a strong, determined voice answered.

"Father!" "Master Hsu!" several voices greeted the newcomer.

"But, Father, what if she dies?" Guei-lung asked.

"There's no other choice, son. She will certainly die without it. For Mei-hua's father, my friend, we must try this solution." He crossed his arms, thrust his hands into his wide sleeves, and said: "Do whatever is necessary, Doctor."

# Chapter 16

SWEEPING HIS LONG ROBE ASIDE, the doctor reached out for his medicine bag. "We can begin immediately. I brought the antidote with me."

Listening to all this, Mei-hua trembled within her frozen body. Her life, or death, was being determined by others. She agreed with Master Hsu. She definitely wanted to try the antidote. This was no way to live for the rest of her life, however long—or short—that life turned out to be. A living death was all she had now. Being able to hear everything going on around her only made her more frustrated with her inability to communicate. Everything must be done to regain her former life—however slim the chances of success.

No one spoke. The sound of porcelain against porcelain rang out as the doctor rapidly mixed medicines in a container. Soon all was quiet.

Mei-hua was frantic to know what was happening. What did the silence mean?

Then: "Hold her head back while I spoon this into her throat. Once we get this liquid into the back of her mouth, her automatic reflexes should cause her to swallow it. Here, hold her head like that. More. All right. She's had enough. Now all we can do is wait."

Mei-hua realized that the doctor's comment meant her body had taken in the antidote, but she had no sensation, felt nothing, tasted nothing. Perhaps that was for the best, she thought. Medicines weren't known for their delicious flavor.

"How long before it takes effect, Doctor?" asked Madam Wu.

"It depends on her. Watch her carefully. If she goes into convulsions, we must keep her from choking on her own tongue. Someone needs to stay with her."

"I'll stay, *ma-ma*," Ping-an quickly said.

"Yes, you and Orchid can stay. No, Guei-lung, you cannot remain. It's not proper for a young man to be here."

"Mother, this is an exceptional situation. I really must remain."

"Guei-lung. Listen to your Mother," his father said. "Your being here will not bring back her health any sooner. Go and check on Mr. Mu. Make sure nothing is given to him except Doctor Lum's medicines, and that they are only administered by Doctor Lum's assistant. Do I make myself clear?"

"Yes, Sir." Guei-lung said unenthusiastically. "And what about food? He needs to eat."

"His wife should make his soup and test it before giving it to him. In case someone has tampered with the food in the house," Doctor Lum said.

"Couldn't one of the servants go instead? I may be needed," Guei-lung tried one last time to remain.

"Don't worry, son. As soon as Mei-hua shows any sign of recovering, we'll send a servant and let you know," Master Hsu said.

Soon the room was quiet once more. Mei-hua lost her last grip on consciousness.

* * *

Blinking, Mei-hua gradually focused on the familiar round face sitting near her.

Ping-an's eyes brightened. "Orchard! She's waking up! Go immediately to tell father and ma-ma."

Within minutes, her parents were standing at her side. Madam Wu bent low over Mei-hua. She took up her hand and gently caressed it with her finger tips, murmuring words of encouragement. Master Hsu stood behind his wife intently watching Mei-hua's face.

Doctor Lum came hurrying into the room, his cloak flying behind him. "Good. Good. She's come around in a short period of time."

Madam Wu moved away to allow the Doctor to examine her more carefully. "Yes, she'll be fine. Her pulse is returning to normal and her eyes are focusing.

"Mei-hua, do you hear me?" he asked, his voice remarkably clear and close.

Mei-hua barely nodded her head. The world around her remained distant and dim. She fought to clear her head, to try and move.

"Take it easy," the doctor cautioned her. "Here," he touched her right hand, "try and move your fingers on this hand."

Concentrating, Mei-hua willed her fingers to move.

"Good. Good. Now try and move your other hand.

"Now your right foot. Can you lift your foot? Good."

The doctor slowly and quietly directed her efforts. After a while, he smiled down at her and said, "Good. You've returned from the gate of death, young lady. My advice now is for you to get a few more days of bed rest and eat light foods, perhaps rice and non-spicy soup only." Rising, he continued, "Yes. Good. I'll come back to see you again tomorrow. Rest until then."

A flood of happiness filled her. Never before had such small gains meant so much. She would not be locked in a motionless body. She would be free once more.

Euphoric, but also exhausted at the effort it took to move, Mei-hua fell asleep again as soon as he left her side.

*　*　*

When Mei-hua next opened her eyes, Master Hsu stood alone at the window, hands behind his back, looking out into the garden. As she focused on his figure, he turned towards her.

"So, you're coming back to us again, finally," he said, smiling.

She tried to grin and nod. Her head barely moved.

"Don't push yourself. You'll be stronger soon enough."

"Why did this happen?" Mei-hua asked haltingly, her voice unsteady.

Master Hsu stepped to her bedside. "Why did this happen?" he repeated. "That's an interesting question for you to ask. Not 'what happened' but 'why.'"

With effort, Mei-hua managed to rise up to a sitting position. "Before, I ... I ..." She paused to regain her strength before saying: "When I appeared to be in a coma, I couldn't move but I had no problem hearing everything around me."

"Ah, so you heard what Doctor Lum said, about being poisoned?"

Mei-hua nodded as she used her right arm to adjust her sitting position and give herself more support. She leaned against the wall.

"'Why' is a very good question. You and Mr. Mu. Two different people, not living in the same household, not in the same business. Just friends. So why you two? Why not Mr. and Mrs. Mu, for example? Or, why not Mr. Mu and Guei-lung?" He stared at the wall above her head.

"It wasn't an accident. You were purposely poisoned."

Mei-hua started to nod, but her throbbing head stopped her. She tried to take a deep breath, but couldn't. An invisible weight crushed her chest and restricted her breathing.

Master Hsu glanced at her before he said, "We need to know what's going on and what's your part in all this. You know," he studied Mei-hua, "there've been so many strange happenings, things that could have occurred by coincidence, but could also be related. The intercepted trip to the temple, for example. Da-shan turning up among the monks sent to Mr. Mu's. He's been at the carpenter's house through your ordeal."

Mei-hua nodded. "Yes. There's got to be a connection. But is it Da-shan? Is it the temple?" She paused, lost in thought, so absorbed in the mystery, she forgot about the proper rules of behavior. She went on,

"The Abbot is well-known as a pious man and he's been at the temple for many, many years. What would drive him to cause all these 'accidents' now? Besides, I hadn't even met him before the other day." She closed her eyes momentarily as a burst of pain shot through her head, then she went on, "Or is it the Taoist priest? I thought his voice was familiar."

Master Hsu raised his eyebrows in a question. Mei-hua pursed her lips, then continued, "In the beginning I thought it reminded me of the robbers' leader's voice, but I can't be sure. No one else seemed to recognize it. And, the idea of either holy man wanting to harm any of us seems so far-fetched anyway."

Master Hsu nodded and rubbed his chin mulling over the problem. "We simply don't have enough information. We need to find out what's happening and who is behind all this. I'll send out my best men to investigate. They'll question everyone who has been to the Mus.'"

"So, you think the Mus are the real targets?" Mei-hua asked.

"Very likely. Everything that has happened seems to tie back to them. We'll get to the bottom of this, but it would be better if we at least knew what we were looking for. We don't even know what's at stake here. What's the motivation behind all this? What do the criminals want?"

"We already know Mr. Mu's in terrible danger," Mei-hua spoke cautiously though the pounding in her head. "If the carpenter's family is at the center of some plot, and your officers saturate the people in the area with questions that could increase the level of danger.

Someone may try to kill them both."

"I'll send a man to protect them, of course. But there's always the potential for things to go wrong."

Master Hsu's hand cupped his chin as he considered what to do. Mei-hua gazed at her quilted cover. The shapes and boldly colored scraps of cloth were arranged with no obvious pattern. She fingered the cloth, absently noting that the stitching holding it all together was invisible.

"Does anyone else know of my recovery?"

"No, no one. Even the doctor questioned whether you were going to actually pull out of this or not. He's been quite cautious."

"In that case, I have an idea. I'll go back to the Mus' house. Go as if I were still in a coma. You could say your mother called in a Taoist priest to see me and he insisted the gods wanted me to be with Mr. Mu. Only they, the gods, had the power to choose which one would die and which would live."

He smiled down at her but said, "No, no. You are brave, as always, but I have an obligation to your Father! I absolutely cannot place you in danger's path again."

"Guei-lung and Soldier Guo will go with me," she went on rapidly, digging deep inside for the strength to speak. "Since they are familiar with the place and people are accustomed to seeing them, no one will be suspicions. Plus, you know," she paused and avoided Master Hsu's eyes as she continued, "it's possible Guei-lung's the target. He was the one the bandits wounded outside the temple. If he's at the Mus' with me, he may be the added enticement for the criminals to tip their hand.

"We can return to the house, appearing to be simply following the Taoist's instructions, but it will be a trap."

Master Hsu remained silent as he thought through what she was suggesting. The plan would put both his son and his charge in danger. The muted *swish-swish-swish* of servants sweeping the veranda outside their window was the only sound in the room for a long time.

Then he said, "This might work, if we're alert, watching for every possible move by the criminals. You and Guei-lung, plus Soldier Guo and a couple of my men, can return to the house. But, no more séances where people are hidden in blankets of smoke! Our only chance is to see the culprit. Let's hope we find him, before he strikes again!"

## CHAPTER 17

MEI-HUA RETURNED to the carpenter's home as if still in a comatose state. Two strong men from Magistrate Hsu's court carried her cot inside. Guei-lung and Soldier Guo hovered near.

The Taoist priest was still there, noisily slurping a bowl of noodles. Mei-hua heard the thick, earthenware bowl hit against wood as he dropped it onto the table. He immediately clapped his hands and ordered, "Place her on the small bed in the corner of Mr. Mu's room."

Mrs. Mu shuffled over from her husband's bedside. "This isn't right." She raised her voice. "She shouldn't be here now. Too many people have started coming to wish my husband good health. Such a young girl shouldn't be exposed to the eyes of strangers."

"It's not up to us. The gods must decide between them—which one will stay and which one will return. Or, if they will both return to this red dust." The Taoist said, as if dismissing her complaint.

"Yes, yes. But it's not right," she maintained. The plaintive note in the older woman's voice touched Mei-hua. Mrs. Mu was always trying to protect her. "We don't have a more private area, I know. Still, she must not be where visitors see her. She's a proper, unmarried girl. It's not right," she repeated yet again.

"I'll tell your husband's well-wishers they aren't allowed in this room. They can visit with you in the shop out front," Guei-lung said.

"That will help," the carpenter's wife said.

"I'll tell you what," The Taoist added thoughtfully. "The gods need to have them close together because they will appear before the netherworld's court together. Nevertheless, we can create privacy for Mei-hua. I'll have my assistant put up a curtained wall between her and the rest of the room. He can do it quickly." After a short time, he added, "She will be fine here, behind such a curtain. The cloth has peaches and pine branches embroidered on it—all symbolizing long life. She is safe and blessed."

"Um-hum," Mrs. Mu said with approval.

The sound of Soldier Guo's boots came closer to Mei-hua.

"No, no. That won't do, soldier," the Taoist said sharply. "You're too close and will interfere with the ritual. Stand over by that window. What do you think you can do anyhow, tackle a spirit?" He laughed and his assistant joined him.

"After we set up our arrangements for inviting the gods to come and make their decision, and just before we are ready for the ceremony, we will push the curtain back. The gods want full view of both Mei-hua and Mr. Mu. At that time, the spirits will make their decision."

"Guei-lung," Mrs. Mu gently addressed the grieving young man, "you sit on this side of Mr. Mu. You will be near him, and at the same time, not too far from

Mei-hua."

"Thank you, Mrs. Mu. I promised Father I would remain to help in whatever way I can." With these words, the soft dragging sound of a stool suggested to Mei-hua that Guei-lung was moving to a spot between Mr. Mu and her curtained area.

"Now that Mei-hua has returned, my assistant and I must prepare for tonight's ceremony. We'll return as soon as we have everything together."

There was so little space in the room that the curtained wall touched the side of her bed. She smiled. This was perfect. Without having to move her head or change position, she was able to create a small separation in the curtain's panels. The slit allowed a clear view of the main room without anyone noticing her. As the Taoist left the room, he briefly stopped to order one of his assistants to stand between the curtain and Soldier Guo. He then requested a second assistant to accompany him. The front door's dull thump told her they had left the shop.

No one spoke while the group waited for the Taoist to return. Mrs. Mu cooked rice and prepared other tasty dishes of vegetables sautéed in oil, onion, and garlic. Whatever other sauces she used, she made sure every dish was slightly sweet. She needed to feed the ghosts as well as the humans, and she wanted the ghosts to think sweet thoughts when making their decisions. Guei-lung sat buried in his own thoughts, motionless, staring with unseeing eyes. The fragrance of cooking and burning incense mixed with the Buddhist monks' prayers surrounded them with a sense of hope and peace.

Before long, the Taoist strode through the door. His arms were full of cloth, bowls, and packages. His assistant followed with more equipment. Without a word to anyone, they set up an altar using a table pushed against the wall adjacent to the one with Mei-hua's bed on it. Over the table, they spread cloth embroidered with Taoist symbols in gleaming red, black, and white thread. With practiced skill, they swiftly and carefully set several statues of local gods, small tablets with ghost writing on them, and pots of various sizes on the cloth. As with earthly bureaucratic ceremonies, precision was important. Each piece on the table had to be exactly correct in its relationship to the others. Any mistake could jeopardize the entire ritual's success.

After arranging the sacred objects and fussing over the exact location and the direction each piece faced, the Taoist ordered his assistant to bring him a large cloth package. The priest loosened his rough cotton outer jacket while his assistant placed the package at his feet and proceeded to untie its many knots in a particular, magical order. Another assistant helped the priest remove his jacket and slip on a long silk over-garment that fell to the tops of his shoes.

Once the sash was tied, the assistant slipped another lustrous, but sleeveless, garment over the first. Mysterious symbols of Taoism—representing the duality of the universe—covered this outer layer, which also touched the tops of his shoes. As with the cloth covering the altar, the symbols were embroidered in brilliant colors of red, yellow, and black. Finally, the assistant securely tied the priest's hair back and placed a hat, full of religious symbols, on his head. The result transformed the priest, making him an unmistakable image of power and authority.

"Master Hsu Guei-lung," the assistant said to the silent figure, "please move your stool to the other side of Mr. Mu's bed. My honorable Master needs this space to address the gods. They are dangerous and he does not wish to place you in danger."

Without a word, Guei-lung moved his stool. He cast a worried glance toward her curtain, but did as he was asked without protest.

"Mrs. Mu," the assistant continued, once Guei-lung had settled down on his stool again, "would you kindly sit next to the young master. It will be too dangerous for you, a weak woman, to be so near your husband. We do not know where the spirits will go or what they will do."

Without pause, she took a stool from near the stove and sat next to Guei-lung. "The food is ready. It's in those bowls," she told the assistant, pointing to several bowls lined up on the side of her stove.

"Good. When we need them, I'll bring them over," the assistant replied without glancing at the pots.

Meanwhile, the priest began to pray. After each set of prayers he lit a stick of incense and placed it into a shiny brass vase in the middle of the altar.

The assistant observed his master for a few minutes, then turned to Guei-lung and Mrs. Mu. "It will be necessary for your servants," his eyes swept over Soldier Guo and the two large men standing near Guei-lung, "to leave the room."

"Sorry, these two can go," Guei-lung answered,

sweeping his arm towards the two male servants, "but, he," pointing at Soldier Guo, "must stay."

"Sir ..."

"He must stay by order of Magistrate Hsu."

"Yes, of course," the assistant quickly agreed at the mention of Magistrate Hsu's name. "In that case, we can perhaps move him over here. Out of harm's way."

Guei-lung seemed about to agree, when Soldier Guo spoke up.

"That's not possible. I either remain here or I'll stand there." He pointed to his original position, immediately next to Mei-hua's curtain.

"Sir, I ask you," the assistant turned to Guei-lung. "Please, help me. Your servant cannot remain where he is."

Guei-lung examined the determined guard, who stood firm, eyes on her curtain. Shrugging his shoulders, he said, "He's here on the magistrate's order. He's not my servant; he's the court's soldier. There isn't anything we can do."

Mei-hua almost grinned at his little speech. Guei-lung pretended to be powerless over Soldier Guo, because then the soldier couldn't be moved. She was glad to have him nearby this time. She was glad to have both of them at her side.

The Taoist priest interrupted shortly: "Its fine. The soldier can stay, if he must. I cannot be responsible for his safety. There's no telling what the gods will do, but certainly the magistrate's orders will be followed. Let him remain." Turning back to his work, he nodded for his assistant to continue.

"It's critical for the three of you to bend your

heads and close your eyes. Do not look up, no matter what you hear. The spirits of the dead are coming soon and they will tear you apart if you see them," the assistant said.

A shiver ran through Mei-hua. *I hope we're doing the right thing*, she thought.

With a quick hand motion, Guei-lung indicated for the two other men to leave. They withdrew to just outside the door, where they remained standing.

Guei-lung, Soldier Guo, and Mrs. Mu bowed their heads. Mei-hua watched this unfold from behind the embroidered cloth's protection. However, as soon as her friends bowed their heads, the assistant moved toward her curtain. Fearing he would see her, she dropped back onto the cot and again lay as if in a coma. The soft sounds of the curtain being pulled back told her she was now exposed.

"Good," the Taoist said in barely a whisper. "Now the two are visible to the sprits and the choice can be made."

She shivered slightly as the air seemed to change and a wave of ice shot through her. She began to doubt the wisdom of her plan. Who knew what was real? What if she was wrong, and the spirits really did control whether she and Mr. Mu died? Who knew whether the boundary between the netherworld and the red dust even existed and, if it did, how thin was it? She willed her body to total stillness, fighting against the trembling which kept rising in her.

The *dun-dun-dun* of a wooden drum, beaten in a steady, unerring rhythm, linked together with the intermittent clang of a brass gong. The prayers would begin soon, following the rhythm set up by these simple instruments. Oddly, the sounds neither clashed nor blended with the Buddhists chanting in the adjoining room. They stood on their own against the Buddhist backdrop of rising and falling voices.

Once more, the assistant warned the three to remain safe from the coming spirits by keeping their heads down and their eyes closed. As if to accent his words, the priest began a prayer pleading with the spirits to remember their mission: to decide which soul they would extract the debt of time. Further, he pointed out that they had no right to take the soul of anyone else in the room. He threatened them with loss of food and complaints to the Emperor of the Dead if they did not listen to him.

Next, the Taoist began a series of prayers in the spirit language. An assistant picked up the prayer; his strong, steady voice kept time with the drum and dominated the room. Another assistant periodically struck the gong, reminding the gods to pay attention and not daydream.

Mei-hua listened absently to his praying. Under all this raucous noise, she heard feet moving steadily about the room and ending near her bed. *Probably the assistant, preparing the next stage of ceremony*, she thought.

Suddenly a strange silence enveloped the prayerful sounds. Within less than a beat, Master Hsu's commanding voice called out, "Stop! You're under arrest!"

Mei-hua's eyes flew open at these words, just in time to catch a glimpse of light glancing off a blade held over her. The blade dropped, aimed at her chest. She instantly began to roll away, instinctively turning out of its path. At the same time, arms encircled her and a heavy body fell on top of her.

"Guo!" she cried as he crushed against her.

Instead of answering, he went limp; his weight pressing her into the cot.

"Get that man!" Magistrate Hsu commanded. "Quick! Before he strikes again!"

The assailant raised the knife up, but the guards were faster. They grabbed him, yanked him back, and held his arms in an iron grip. The blade clattered to the floor. Caught, immobile, he stopped resisting. He slumped in their grasp, gasping in defeat.

Guei-lung tugged at Soldier Guo, rolling him off of Mei-hua. He lay still next to her on the cot. She didn't have to ask what happened. The sticky wetness of blood seeped through the bedding. Soldier Guo had protected her from a vicious attack by taking the knife in his own back.

With Guei-lung's help, Mei-hua carefully wriggled free, trying not to disturb or move the unconscious soldier.

"Leave him there," Master Hsu said. Then, turning towards his two guards, he ordered, "Pick the cot up and take it to the residence. Get a doctor immediately!"

After watching the men carry the young soldier out of the shop, Mei-hua gazed back at the now harmless, would-be assailant. She found herself looking into the face of the Taoist priest. Shocked, she cried out in dismay, "Aiya!"

She never expected such callousness, such cynical manipulation of people's trust and beliefs. She peeked quickly at the carpenter's wife to see how she was reacting. Would she think this wretched turn of events endangered her husband even more? Or would she understand that the entire ritual was a false front for the criminals?

The answer was short in coming.

Mrs. Mu rose from her seat as if possessed. Anger colored her face a deep red and made her voice hoarse.

"You bad egg! You piece of scorched earth! Beetle dung! How dare you try to murder Mei-hua and destroy my husband?" She flew from across the room toward the cornered priest.

Just as her hands were about to tear at his face, Master Hsu reached out and held her back. "Mrs. Mu, I will see to it that you and your husband get justice. Please, don't burden yourself with his bad blood."

Mrs. Mu strained against his hold on her.

"Madam!"

Finally, she collapsed in his grasp and sobbed, tears streaming down her withered cheeks.

# CHAPTER 18

MAGISTRATE HSU LED Mrs. Mu to a stool near her husband and steadied her as she sat. She bent her head near him, silent in her pain, and gently placed a hand on her husband's still frame. Hsu spun around and, pointing to the Taoist, ordered, "Take him into custody!"

Two guards with ample girth and bulging muscles grabbed the scoundrel and began dragging him through the room.

"No! Wait! This is a mistake!" the stricken Taoist screamed, his face white, his eyes bulging. "I'm not the one! Do not take me!" He jerked his arms, struggling against the guards' steely grip.

All of his flailing about was like pulling against a knot in a rope. The more he tried to free himself, the tighter they held him.

"Guards, keep him still. I want to talk to him," Hsu ordered.

"Yes, yes," the Taoist quickly responded, smiling obsequiously at the magistrate. Then, flashing an angry look at the guards, he attempted to pull his arms free once more.

"They're not going to release you. Pay attention and stop thrashing about," Hsu said coldly.

Turning to Mei-hua, he continued in a lowered voice, "Are you well enough to come with me to the office? We must interrogate the Taoist before he gathers his wits about him and protects the ones who put him up to this scheme. I've no doubt he works for someone else. I'll need about an hour to question him and then we can all meet."

"Yes, Sir. I'm fine." There was no way Mei-hua would miss a chance to discover what was behind this bizarre case. Even if she were dying, she'd still come.

"Bring him along!" Magistrate Hsu called out to the guards as he strode to the door.

"No, no!" the priest screamed. In terror of the certain torture he faced during interrogation, he quivered in fear, blubbering almost incoherently. "It's Mr. Mien, the noodle vendor. We worked together to drive Mr. and Mrs. Mu out of business."

Mei-hua glanced at Magistrate Hsu as he swung around and faced the Taoist. So she had been right to distrust the smarmy man. Mr. Mien was a part of a plot to kill his neighbor, all the while pretending to help. She realized he was in the perfect spot to destroy the Mus because he was always here. He was trusted. Mrs. Mu did whatever he suggested.

Clearly, in his panic, the Taoist wanted to reveal everything. There was no time to wait until they took him to the official interrogation room. They needed to act immediately. Arrests had to be made before the others involved were alerted and fled.

Mei-hua caught Magistrate Hsu's attention. He nodded as if he read her thoughts.

"Guards, bring the worm before me," he

thundered.

As the guards flung the quivering man down at his feet, Master Hsu's eyes burned in anger at the sight of such a despicable character. After a long pause, during which the prisoner seemed to shrink in size, the magistrate called out: "Speak!"

Mei-hua watched as the Taoist, who just a short time ago had been arrogantly manipulating them all, now dropped to his knees and groveled on the floor.

"Your honor," he began, whimpering. "I am an innocent victim. Mr. Mien forced me to comply with his wishes. He threatened me. If I didn't help him drive the Mus out of this building, he would have certain associates of his come and break my bones." He pleaded with a look at the magistrate, then at Mei-hua and the others. "You understand. If I didn't help, he would have done it. I have no doubt."

"And so you contrived to murder Mr. Mu to save your own skin," boomed the magistrate.

"No, not to murder." He rose up in a panic. "Never!" His face lost its color and he anxiously hurried his story. "I was to make him sick, so he would lose his business and sell out cheaply to the noodle vendor. That's all. I ..."

"That's all? Why did you try to kill Mei-hua just now? Tell the truth! What has that to do with selling the shop?" the magistrate thundered.

The Taoist fell forward onto the floor, beseeching the judge, "Please, Your Honor. It wasn't me ..."

"Wasn't you? You attacked her before our very eyes. Do you take the court for a fool? Speak or there will be no leniency!"

The terrorized man looked up. "I was ordered to. I planned to kill her earlier, but when you removed her to your home, I thought I'd lost my chance," he began to spill out his tale. "Then, when she returned, I knew I had no choice; I had to finish her off. Even though it may appear foolhardy, I had no choice. There was no time for a more elaborate plan. You could take her back at any time."

"So, you tried to stab her to death, knowing you would be captured and taken to court?" Hsu asked.

"Yes and no. I expected to kill her and also die myself, not be arrested."

Mei-hua stared at the groveling priest, her erstwhile murderer. Before she'd thought he'd been so imposing, in command, a leader. Now, he appeared deflated, a sad, sorry resemblance of his former self. She felt no anger, nor sympathy. Only relief at being alive.

Magistrate Hsu drew his brows together and frowned at the man. "You are a coward," he said coldly. "Arrest meant certain torture and a punishment of decapitation or dismemberment. This death is easy in comparison, but you should accept and take responsibility for your crimes before the law."

Mei-hua nodded. It was brutal, but—as today— just the fear of pain drove many to confess.

"Tell the court who was behind all this. I don't believe it was Mr. Mien all by himself. He may be a part of it, but he's not the mastermind. Who are you really working for? Who is so powerful that you are willing to die to carry out his orders?"

"Honorable Sir, I ..."

At that moment something shot through the room and struck the Taoist in the forehead. He lurched backward and toppled over. He was dead.

"What ..." "Who ..." "Where did ..." everyone yelled at once. Mei-hua caught a glimpse of a crossbow disappearing from the window.

"Over there! At the window!" she called to the guards. But she knew, even as they ran out of the house into the street, it was too late. Whoever had killed the Taoist was already gone. It was easy to slip away and to hide in such a crowded and congested area. It was useless. They would never discover the anonymous assailant.

"Mr. Mien! We must find him right away," she urgently said to the magistrate. He gave a curt nod and ordered the remaining guards to find the noodle vendor and take him to jail where he could be safely interrogated.

Mei-hua stared at the dead man crumpled on the floor like so much old paper, and wondered if it was already too late to find the noodle seller. Would Mr. Mu's enemy escape, too?

# CHAPTER 19

MEI-HUA AND GUEI-LUNG didn't have to wait long after returning to their home before Master Hsu's servant arrived with a message. He began by letting them know that Soldier Guo's wound was taken care of and he would recover without permanent injury. Then he went on to inform them that Mr. Mien was in custody. He would appear before the court in the morning. The magistrate wanted him to spend the night in jail surrounded by instruments of torture used in interrogating difficult prisoners. It would give the noodle vendor time to consider his options. The messenger ended by saying that Mei-hua and Guei-lung could come to court tomorrow to hear his deposition.

Mei-hua spent a restless night and jumped out of bed at the first signs of light to prepare to go to court. Slipping on her outer jacket, she stepped out into the courtyard and was pleased to find Guei-lung, pacing the garden, waiting for her. His mother, already dressed, sat on a nearby bench. The rising sun picked up the sheen on her fine peach-colored silk overcoat embroidered with bats and other symbols of good luck and success. She smiled at her young charge.

"Good morning, Auntie," Mei-hua greeted her.

She guessed why the elegant woman was there in the garden, waiting for her. Madam Mu was responsible for the household. It was her duty to be sure everything was proper and in order. As a woman and member of the Hsu household, Mei-hua could not be exposed to the public.

"Stay behind the screen at the back of the court. You will be able to hear and see everything from there. Guei-lung will accompany you and remain with you," Guei-lung's mother said.

"Yes, Ma'am. Have you heard anything about whether Mrs. Mu will be there?"

"She will stay home and care for her husband. That will comfort them both."

"Yes, of course. Hearing the noodle vendor's testimony this morning may be upsetting." Mei-hua looked down, a frown on her face as she thought of the carpenter's wife. She was always so trusting. This turn of events had to be deeply troubling.

"Don't worry, Mei-hua. I'll make sure both Mrs. and Mr. Mu are tended to. Go along and don't worry about them," she repeated.

Mei-hua smiled a thank you while bowing to her. She knew that her friends were in safe hands under Madam Wu's care. Quickly, she and Guei-lung left the garden and hurried through the residence to the court.

Magistrate Hsu was already interrogating Mr. Mien as they slipped behind the courtroom's screen. The prisoner, still wearing his greasy apron, seemed to have shrunk as he knelt before the judge, hands tied behind his back.

Mei-hua took up a position where the prisoner

was clearly visible. He never lifted his stare from the floor immediately in front of him. If he, as a prisoner, had looked directly at the magistrate, it would have been considered an act of pure arrogance. Whether he felt it or not, his posture—kneeling with his eyes down—made him appear remorseful. Mei-hua wondered if he really was sorry. Did he have any sense of guilt for what he had done to the elderly couple?

"Go on, continue. Tell everything, as it happened," the magistrate barked.

"Well, you see, as I said, I have had only a noodle stall for two years, right outside the Mu shop. Ching Da, the leader of the local secret society, came to me one day and made an offer. The secret society needed a place to operate out of, someplace that was discreet, where they could come on a regular basis and not attract attention. A noodle shop suited their purposes. And then, too, they wanted one close to the magistrate's offices."

"Why? What was the reason behind choosing such a location?" the magistrate interrupted.

Trembling, the kneeling man replied quickly, "I don't know, your honor." He ducked his head as if anticipating a blow from the nearby guard and hastily continued, "They never told me why. I thought it odd myself. Perhaps they thought the law would never look for them so close to the court itself. I cannot say. I only know the location was important.

"Being a poor merchant, I have to sell to whoever comes to my stall. I did not seek them out," he whined. Mei-hua shook her head. He wanted the magistrate to think he was nothing more than an unwilling pawn of the gang.

"Continue," the magistrate said abruptly.

"Yes, well, they came to me and said they could help me find a place for a real noodle shop, not just a stall for me anymore. I told them I wasn't interested, because I couldn't afford a shop even if I could find one to rent.

"They told me not to worry; they would finance my business. All I had to do was run the noodle shop in front, while they had their meetings in the back.

"Mr. Mu's carpenter shop was in the ideal location. It would be my noodle shop. But I told them such a plan was impossible. The carpenter would never sell. The place had been in his family for generations and he needed to work to live, too." He glanced up at the Judge, a look of expectation on his face. *Did he think this claim made him less guilty?* Mei-hua wondered. She caught Guei-lung's eye. They shook their heads.

The magistrate remained silent, waiting.

Gathering himself up, the noodle vendor went on, "They laughed and said if I did exactly what they told me, in a short time the Mus would sell their place to me and be glad to do it." The prisoner raised his eyes to the magistrate's feet and whimpered, "I had to do what they wanted. Even you, the arm of the law, would not be able to protect me from such lawless men! I had no choice!"

"What did they tell you to do? Again, be very specific; don't leave anything out," Hsu demanded, ignoring his questions.

Mien nodded, dropped his gaze again, and said, "They gave me a poison to put into a bowl of noodle soup and make sure Mr. Mu ate it. Only gave it to the carpenter, not his wife. Her soup was fine. By poisoning his soup a little each day, it would look like he was sick. He would not be able to work and his expenses would rapidly build up. Eventually, they would have to sell his shop to pay for his doctor and medicine, or even for his funeral. But if Mrs. Mu also died, people might get suspicious, so she was never supposed to be harmed.

"Planting a doctor, and even a Taoist priest, in the house was easy. Once Mrs. Mu trusted me, I could get her to do almost anything, if I said it would help her husband. Of course, each thing I came up with brought him closer to bankruptcy and closer to death. It was masterful." Pride at the brilliance of their plan snuck into his voice. He quickly glanced over at the guard and up at the Judge.

"But then, Mei-hua got involved." A slight bitterness replaced the brief glimpse of pride he'd just expressed. "When she and Guei-lung turned up at the shop, I was afraid that would ruin everything. I wanted to stop, to flee the city, but Ching Da threatened me again. He scorned my fear. He said his boss would take care of those two insects."

"Did he name the boss?" the Judge asked.

"No. I never knew his name. But it's somebody high up, somebody important. Ching Da seemed to think his boss could protect us from anything, anything." He paused, pressed his hand momentarily over his eyes, then continued. "Ching Da set up the ambush against Guei-lung and Mei-hua on the way to the temple."

When Mei-hua heard this, she gasped. So, it was

not a mere coincidence. But how could anyone have known about their temple trip? The arrangements were made at the last minute. Before she could consider other possibilities, the noodle vendor continued.

"When that failed to stop them from interfering, Ching Da's boss developed another plan involving the Taoist, Mei-hua, and the spirit ceremony. That one looked foolproof once Mei-hua agreed to go along with it for the carpenter's sake."

"How did they know about the temple trip, or about Mei-hua and Guei-lung staying with the Mus?" Magistrate Hsu asked.

"I don't know. Ching Da seemed to know everything. Almost before something happened, he knew about it. I told you, his boss is somebody important and has lots of connections. He knew everything."

Mei-hua glanced at Magistrate Hsu. He raised his eyebrows and nodded his head toward the screen. Then he said what Mei-hua was thinking: "Clearly, someone inside the court has been giving information to Ching Da or his boss. Who is this person? You must know something! Speak up or I will have no choice but to have the guards make you talk!"

In terror, the noodle vendor rapidly beat his head on the floor, trying to bow, but unable to with his hands tied behind his back. "Honorable Sir! Have mercy! I am telling you all I know! If it came from someone inside the court, I don't know who it is! Ching Da never told me about the boss; he only told me what to do and when to do it. Please believe me, I would tell you if I could!" Again, the frightened man knocked his head on the floor, attempting to bow before the judge.

Realizing he had gotten as much information as he could out of the guilty man, Magistrate Hsu shouted, "Guard, remove the prisoner and take him into jail to wait further action."

No sooner had the noodle vendor been taken out of the room, when a soldier came in to report that Ching Da and the rest of the gang members named by Mr. Mien had all disappeared, as if swallowed up by the city.

Mei-hua sighed and cast a long look at Guei-lung.

"How could they have vanished so quickly?" Guei-lung asked under his breath.

"Uncle is right, this has to be the work of an insider," Mei-hua responded equally quietly. "Someone who knows the courts and has access to private information, maybe even private conversations. How could the courts be infiltrated by secret society members? What and, most importantly, who is behind this?"

There were only questions, no answers, as they stood unseen behind the screen wondering and watching the guards and clerks' faces.

# CHAPTER 20

"GUARDS, CLEAR THE COURTROOM! Everyone must be removed," the Judge ordered. At the magistrate's commands, the large room immediately emptied. Even the soldiers left, taking up their post outside the entrance. After the last person left and the guard firmly closed the massive carved wooden doors, he turned toward the elaborate screen and said, "Mei-hua and Guei-lung, come here."

They emerged and moved closer to him. He beckoned them to follow him into his inner office where they sat in a close circle. They could discuss events without anyone who might be standing outside the windows or doors overhearing.

"We've discovered the person immediately responsible for Mr. Mu's sickness," Guei-lung's father began, "and who tried to harm you two in the temple incident. The Taoist priest is dead; his assistants have been arrested. Mr. Mien is in jail and we have warrants out for the arrest of the gang leader, Ching Da, and his men.

"With this, Mr. Mu and his wife are safe. Under the care of our medical doctor, it is just a matter of time before Mr. Mu regains his health and can resume work.

There shouldn't be further trouble for them.

"Technically, the case is closed. But," here he paused and leaned forward, hands together, his index fingers forming an inverted V. He gazed long and hard at his son and Mei-hua before continuing. "Clearly these incidents are part of a larger pattern. This larger pattern raises other questions: Who is the 'boss'? What does he want? What is his ultimate goal? How do you two fit into it, if, in fact, you do?"

Mei-hua raised her head, "Are you suggesting our being attacked was not a result of our trying to help the Mus?"

"It's possible," the magistrate admitted, "you were simply pawns in the overall game to take over Mr. Mu's shop. However, it's also possible you two were a separate target."

Wiping his hand across his forehead, the magistrate said, "What troubles me the most is that someone knew you were going to the temple. Knew almost as soon as we decided you should go. How could that have happened?"

"Someone within the house or from within the courts is passing on information," Mei-hua suggested, her voice just a whisper.

"Yes, as disturbing as it may be, I'm afraid that is the most reasonable explanation," Magistrate Hsu said.

"Then the issue becomes: Who spied on us?" Guei-lung interjected. "But who had reason to act against us?" He swept a hand over the two of them as they sat in front of the Judge.

Mei-hua nodded. If they were the targets, that

alone raised more unanswerable questions. How could they influence anything? They were both too young to hold official positions. What could they do?

Just then, a guard entered.

"What do you want?" the magistrate barked. "I specifically gave orders not to be disturbed!"

"Sir, I have an urgent message for you concerning Soldier Guo."

Mei-hua started. A thought that had been eating at her, but which remained tucked away in the back of her mind, began to move forward. And still she didn't want to consider its possibility.

"Enter and report."

The guard bowed perfunctorily at the door, strode across the room, and murmured to the magistrate. Even though Mei-hua strained to hear, she couldn't tell what was being said. When the guard finished, the magistrate waved him away.

He waited a few moments—until after the guard left the room and closed the door—before speaking.

"Soldier Guo has left."

"What?" Guei-lung sat up straight, confusion written on his face.

"Is he all right?" Mei-hua asked. "Where is he?"

"His father sent men to take him home."

"His father?" Mei-hua said.

"Yes. Remember, he is the adopted son of the great eunuch, Lord Chiu. Upon hearing of his son's injuries, he sent a contingent of soldiers to remove the young man to his own chambers near the Palace Compound."

Rubbing his hand over his face once more, he

said, "It would be impossible to prove, but I am sure this young man is our spy."

Mei-hua felt her heart jump. What she feared most, but which she herself could not shake, was just this. Guo was the informer!

"He's the only new member of the household or court staff, and he was present when we discussed how to proceed with the Mus and decided on your going to the temple," Guei-lung said, watching her carefully. "He certainly would've had access to our plans. Plus, he had plenty of time to notify someone on the outside of when we were leaving."

Mei-hua tried to suppress the rising sensation that he was guilty of trying to harm, perhaps kill, not only her but also Guei-lung and Mr. Mu. The pressure in her head kept her from thinking straight. The image of his smiling face and dancing dark eyes flashed before her. There must be a mistake. How could the person who was stabbed trying to save her be one of the people plotting against them? Is it possible to be so wrong about a person? The deception of the Mus' neighbor, the noodle vendor, instantly sprang to mind. Her stomach churned. She thought she'd be sick. The sense of betrayal encompassed her physically as well as mentally.

"Yes," Magistrate Hsu's voice cut through her mental fog, "he had knowledge and opportunity. And as the adopted son of eunuch Chiu, he may have had motive. His first duty was to his uncle."

At Mei-hua's questioning look, he continued: "It is common knowledge that the eunuch Lord Chiu established a vast spy network within the government structure, including its courts. From what I understand, he's claimed he needs the spy network to diligently oversee any wrong-doing on the part of government officials. This is for the protection of our Esteemed Emperor. Of course, at the same time, he also gains information he has effectively used against others for his own purposes.

"In this case, it is possible Guo felt it his duty to his adopted father to be an informer, which meant reporting whatever happened within these chambers and within the court. As his son, it was his filial responsibility. I'm afraid the law upholds this principal. Nothing supersedes one's filial duty in the eyes of the law. I suspected this was the reason behind his being assigned to my office in the first place. So, it may be that he was only doing what he had been sent to do. In that case, the court cannot prosecute him. And then," he paused and tapped his chin, "he may not have fully realized the impact of the information he passed on to others."

"How can you come to his defense, if you really believe he was the spy?" Guei-lung challenged his father, unhappy with his defense of the soldier.

"Look at the circumstances, Guei-lung. Say knowing our decisions and your movements, he informed Lord Chiu's office. Somewhere the information got into the wrong hands—it can happen there as well as here—and the secret society arranged to attack you on the way to the temple. Whatever the case, it is troublesome for us. What I want you both to remember, however, is how Soldier Guo behaved when the gang attacked. He protected Mei-hua and saved you, my son, from death's door. Now he is severely wounded again in defending Mei-hua. So, I must conclude he was not involved in the group trying to harm either of you. His actions suggest he didn't even know of the attack beforehand."

"Does that mean you are not going to have him brought into court for questioning?" Guei-lung bristled.

"That's right. The law wouldn't support such action. Plus, I don't believe he could add anything to what we already know. As I've said, if he acted as a spy for his father, it is not a crime in the eyes of the law. Even if it were, his father represents the Emperor and would claim his son merely carried out the trust placed in him to make sure all arms of the government were honest." He gave them a tired smile. "It would be impossible to obtain a warrant for Guo's arrest. He is too well protected by his father's shadow.

"For now, the leader behind all this is unknown. Or, at least beyond our reach."

While he didn't say it, Mei-hua suspected he meant the powerful Lord Chiu. If he was behind all this ... She dared not think of the serious implications—for her, her father, and the Hsu family. Whoever it was, clearly the danger to her and those dear to her was not over.

Magistrate Hsu straightened his shoulders and continued, "We have Mr. Mien in custody and will continue looking for Ching Da and the others involved." He pressed his lips together in a frustrated gesture. "In the meantime, I will keep my promise to your father, Mei-hua: we must and will keep you safe within the walls of our home."

Mei-hua stole a peek at Guei-lung standing tall

and handsome, so close at hand. In spite of the seriousness of the situation, a flutter of happiness filled her. Being confined to the Hsu household had its advantages.

**THE END**

## Author's Note: Mei-hua's World

WHILE THIS STORY AND ITS CHARACTERS are fiction, I tried to be as true to the time Mei-hua lived as possible. The situations in which Mei-hua and her friends find themselves reflect what could have happened given the culture and society of the time. Their solutions also reflect what was available to them and was commonly considered to be appropriate.

Medical Problems

*Guei-lung's injured arm*

When people had a broken arm or wound, the medical procedure was usually simple and straightforward. Anyone with basic medical training, such as a bell-doctor (also known as a folk or local street doctor), could take care of the injury. Buddhist monks in some larger temples also had medical knowledge and treated such patients.

*Mr. Mu's illness*

On the other hand, something as simple as a common cold or as challenging as a long-term illness would require a range of options in search of the best medical care. Home remedies involving particular foods would be the first level of attack.

Foods are divided into three groups: hot, cold, and neutral. The idea of hot and cold in this case does not refer to temperature, but rather how the food affects the body. Cold foods have a calming, cooling influence, and thus can bring down temperatures, relieve headaches, and reduce pulse rates. In contrast, hot foods have an energizing influence. They improve circulation, help alleviate stomach pains, and reduce bloating. Ideally, the body should be in balance, neither too hot nor too cold. If the body is too hot, the person should eat more cold foods, such as bamboo shoots and bitter melon, and not hot foods, such as meat, onion, and garlic. If the person's system is cold, he should eat more meat and fewer vegetables. Rice is a neutral food, so people can eat as much rice as they want without harmful effects.

This is why the carpenter's wife felt it was so important for her husband to eat the noodle vendor's noodle and pork soup. The pork would increase his energy level and make him better. The noodles would have been made of rice, a neutral food, which the carpenter could eat as much of as he liked. Also, the noodles themselves had symbolic value due to their shape. They are long and thus regarded as a physical manifestation of a long life. So, the combination of noodles and pork made this particular soup an extremely good choice for the ill carpenter.

If home remedies didn't work, the next level most people would have available to them would be the bell-doctors. These were medical specialists who walked the streets ringing a bell to let potential clients know they were in the area. Bell-doctors trained through apprenticeships, meaning that each person acquired different areas and levels of expertise, depending on what their mentors knew. This was a highly individualized field, and a specialist in one area might not know much or anything about other healing therapies and techniques.

By the Ming Dynasty, there was another well-developed type of medical specialist available: the imperially trained doctor. These men were highly educated and had passed a series of exams in a variety of medical specialties. They were considered to be intellectual and held the highest degree of status among all the medical specialists.

*Causes behind medical problems*

While treating the immediate physical symptoms of an injury, illness, or disease was important, people also wanted to know *why* something happened. That is, why did Mr. Mu get sick and not his wife or someone else? To say a patient had simply tripped and fallen, was bitten by an insect, caught a bad cold on a rainy day, or contracted an illness through exposure to a sick person didn't answer that question. To explain *why* someone came to harm, people looked to the supernatural and to the individual's fate or karma. The interplay of the natural and supernatural worlds was real and ever present.

In *Warned*, looking for supernatural reasons behind the carpenter's illness would have been considered not only appropriate, but necessary. This is especially true given that he keeps getting weaker, nearly to the point of death. Problems arise when unscrupulous characters take advantage of the patient and his family. The great majority of Taoist (also spelled Daoist) priests and Buddhist monks were conscientious and truly carried out the tenets of their spiritual beliefs. Nevertheless, within any group, charlatans can be found, preying on trusting believers at a time they are most vulnerable.

The Eight Immortals

Immortals are beings who once lived as humans on earth, but now inhabit the upper stratum (sometimes called Heaven or celestial level). They have supernatural powers, can assume human shape, and are able to do anything people do—including eating and drinking.

The Eight Immortals were well-known figures by the Ming Dynasty, and remain important Taoist figures today. Even the number eight itself holds great symbolic significance. Specifically, it represents the stages and conditions of human life: age (young and old), status (low and high), fortune (poor and wealthy), and gender (male and female). The Immortals, therefore, include among their number men and women, young and old, rich and poor, simple and educated. As with humans, they have frailties as well as strengths, and can both enjoy and abuse worldly delights. In this story, the immortal Iron Crutch Li (Li Tie-guai) reveals his knowing, benevolent nature by descending to earth in order to warn Mei-hua. And yet he also enjoys his liquor a little too much—which is why he appears carrying a gourd filled with wine. Similarly,

Lan Cai-he, who also comes to warn her, holds castanets because he loves to sing and dance. These two immortals help Mei-hua by alerting her to danger, but they do not solve her problems for her. For, while immortals and other spirits might play powerful roles in the world of Ming China, they did not control human behavior or determine a person's destiny. Instead, supernatural beings operated as additional, influential actors who needed to be watched for, guarded against, or listened to.